The Jackson MacKenzie Chronicles

DOUBLE ENVELOPMENT

By
Angel Giacomo

**1st Battalion
Publishing**

Copyright ©

First publication in 2022 by 1st Battalion Publishing.
1stbattalionpublishing@gmail.com

ISBN 978-1-7345674-7-2

https://thejacksonmackenziechronicles.godaddysites.com

Printed in the United States of America

First Edition: 2022

DISCLAIMER-FICTION

Other than actual historical events and public figures, all characters and incidents portrayed in this novel are fictitious. Any resemblance to actual persons, living or dead, is purely coincidental.

DEDICATION

This book is dedicated to all who have served in every branch of the military. I write it with extreme humility. It is to honor the veterans of the United States who fought in our conflicts, both past, present, and future.

 "No man is a leader until he is ratified in the minds and hearts of his men." — The Soldier's Handbook

"Motivation is the art of getting people to do what you want them to do because they want to do it." — Dwight D. Eisenhower

"America must win this war. Therefore I will work, I will save, I will sacrifice, I will endure, I will fight cheerfully and do my utmost, as if the issue of the whole struggle depended on me alone." — Private Martin A. Treptow, 168th Infantry, 42nd Division, U.S. Army – WWI.

"The ultimate measure of a man is not where he stands in moments of comfort and convenience, but where he stands at times of challenge and controversy." — Dr. Martin Luther King

ACKNOWLEDGMENT

Thank you to those who have believed in me.

Thank you to Dr. Russell W. Ramsey – Lt. Colonel, U.S. Army (retired) USMA 1957 – 8th Regiment, 1st Cavalry Division –Vietnam – 1965-66, for being my friend. Hooah! Go Army! Beat Navy!

An additional shout out to William B. Fuller – U.S. Army, Sergeant, 5th Battalion, 7th Regiment, 1st Cavalry Division – Vietnam – December 1968-69.

Hooah!

CHAPTER 1

1300 Hours
May 10, 1969
Walker Cemetery
Ft. Hood, TX

U.S. Army Major Christopher "Chris" Patterson and his wife, Kara, stood under a black umbrella in front of a small mound of black earth on a gray, overcast, rainy afternoon. The day matched their mood.

At the head of the grave was a temporary white wooden cross with the name Amanda Elizabeth Patterson – Born – May 3, 1969, Died May 3, 1969. The permanent pink granite headstone topped by a winged angel wouldn't be set for two to three months.

Why did God take their baby girl from them before she had a chance to live? He wanted to see his daughter grow up, play with dolls, wear frilly pink dresses, go to high school, the prom, and have a life. While he wanted a boy to carry on the family legacy at West Point, even picking out a name, Donald Eric, he was equally happy with a little girl to spoil.

Chris pulled his wife close to his body as the rain fell harder, splashing from the ground onto the pants of his green class A dress uniform, making the woolen cloth smell like a wet dog. He didn't care. It fit with the gloom of the setting.

"Honey, why did the cord prolapse? I did everything the doctor told me. Why did our little girl die?" Kara asked, tears streaming down her cheeks with her black dress and nylon stockings getting the same treatment as his uniform. She laid her head on his shoulder. They fit perfectly together with both of them being six feet tall.

"I don't know. I wish I did." Chris stroked her long, silky dark-brown hair. A few of the loose strands tickled his nose. He bit his tongue not to sneeze.

"What do we do now? The doctor said I can't have any more children," she mumbled into his shoulder.

"We go on. It's all we can do. I love you. That's all that matters." Chris gripped the envelope in his jacket pocket with his free hand. He didn't want to tell her this. Not here. Not now. But he had no choice. "Kara," he started.

"Yes." She pushed away to look him in the eyes. Her brown eyes flashed with concern. "I don't like the sound of your voice. Is something wrong? What are you not telling me."

"Ahh…I'm no longer in charge of the training for the 13th Support Brigade." A job he really didn't want anyway. Chris pulled the envelope out of his pocket and handed it to her. "My orders came in this morning."

"Orders for what?"

Chris didn't want to say this even though it was his second combat tour in Southeast Asia and his third overall. The first tour was in the Korean War with the 3rd Infantry Division. His last one was with the 82nd Airborne. "Vietnam. I have to leave in two days. I added twenty-five thousand dollars to my life insurance on top of my combat pay. I'm being transferred to the 1st Cavalry Division in the1st Battalion, 7th Cavalry." He could finally use his training and experience instead of sitting on his ass behind a desk doing paperwork.

Maybe he would finally get to thank his West Point roommate, Major Jackson MacKenzie, for introducing him to Kara at the Ft. Bragg officers Christmas party two years ago. Until that day, he never believed in love at first sight. A couple of weeks later, the Army transferred him to the 13th Support Brigade at Ft. Hood, TX, to train replacements. A job he really didn't want. A few weeks later, Kara moved into an apartment off-base, dropping everything and finding another job to be with him. That's when he knew she was his soul mate.

He wanted Jackson to be his best man at his wedding last August, but Jackson was currently deployed in Vietnam with the 5th Special Forces and hadn't replied to his letters. The way the army mail service works, Jackson may have never received them. His second choice, Captain Harry Russell, was also deployed in the same unit.

Kara gripped his hand tightly. "Wasn't the 7th Cavalry General Custer's unit?"

A bit surprised, Chris couldn't help but laugh. "Yeah, it was." *It's also Colonel Moore's unit.* He was in Special Forces training when the Battle of the Ia Drang Valley happened. The first major battle between the United States Army and the People's Army of Vietnam near Chu Pong Massif in the central highlands of Vietnam. Everyone knew about the bravery of the 7th Cavalry Regiment. The Seventh First.

"Don't let Vietnam be your Little Bighorn." Kara kissed his cheek. Her bloodshot eyes and flushed completion demonstrated how much she disagreed with him being deployed. "And I'd rather have you than the money."

2

"Same here." Chris gripped her hand as they walked back to the car. He looked over his shoulder at their daughter's grave, hoping he wouldn't be joining her soon.

CHAPTER 2

0800 Hours
May 15, 1969
1st Cavalry Division Headquarters
(The First Team)
Phước Vĩnh, South Vietnam
III Corps

Chris tucked Kara's picture into his pocket, straightened his pressed and starched ripstop OD green cotton jungle fatigue shirt, and marched into the office of the 7th Cavalry Regiment's commanding officer, Colonel Nathan Best. He stopped in front of the desk and stood at attention. "Major Patterson reporting as ordered, sir."

Colonel Best looked up from the report in his hands. "At ease, Major. Have a seat."

Chris sat in the chair next to him. "Yes, sir." He sized Best up – the man appeared to be in good shape but not overly tall. He looked about five foot six or seven. It was hard to tell with him sitting down. Clean-shaven. What hair the man had was gray and short. He probably didn't go to the barber much or did it himself. He seemed the type.

Quickly, Chris glanced around the office. Overall, it was typical of most platoon, battalion, and regimental offices in Vietnam, barren except for the standard desk, file cabinet, and a few chairs, along with combat gear and weapons staged for quick retrieval.

"I've read your service record, Patterson." The colonel picked up a folder on the desktop. "Impressive. Deputy Brigade Commander at West Point. Top ten percent of your class in 1957. Airborne qualified, Special Forces qualified, Combat Infantry Badge, 2nd award, Bronze Star with Valor device in Korea. Silver Star, Soldier's Medal, Purple Heart, Meritorious Service, and two Army Commendations with Valor device during your previous tour in Vietnam."

"Thank you, sir." What else could he say? The medals didn't show his ability as a soldier, only someone else's opinion of it.

Best held up his right hand. On the ring finger, a unique gold ring with the blue infantry stone in the center. "Class of 1949. We ring knockers need to stick together."

"Yes, sir." *Might come in handy one day if I screw the pooch.*

"As you know, you'll be joining the 1st Battalion. Here's what they didn't tell you. You're the new CO. At least until I find someone with the experience to replace you. For now, you'll remain a major but have the responsibilities of a Lieutenant Colonel. You've got a great bunch of Troopers. Battle-hardened and tough. Treat them with respect, and they'll respond in kind."

That's how he always treated his men. He led from the front. Only douchebags barked out orders from the rear and rolled the dice on getting fragged. "Yes, sir."

"The personnel files on your men are in your office. It's down the hall. Any questions?"

"No, sir."

"Then you are dismissed, Major Patterson."

"Yes, sir." Patterson stood, saluted the colonel, and left the office. He found his office quickly with his name written in black marker on a strip of masking tape stuck to the door. Inside he found his executive officer from Ft. Hood, Captain Carl Jefferson, a young black man who went to OCS after graduating from Grambling University, stacking files on the desk.

The kid had great instincts during field training. Jefferson's only flaw, no combat experience. He was a green as grass newbie who came up through the ranks in supply. But that would come soon with him now in Vietnam, which had no "front" lines. The Viet Cong were everywhere. Even the "vetted" locals who washed their clothes, cleaned their offices, and shined their boots.

Jefferson held up a folder. "Ready for you, Major. All files in alphabetical order."

Just like someone from supply, all organized and efficient.

Patterson sat in the chair behind his desk in the white-walled unadorned office and picked up the top folder in the first stack. "Then sit, Captain. Let's get to work getting to know these men."

CHAPTER 3

0700 Hours
June 1, 1969
Biên Hòa Province, South Vietnam
III Corps

Chris held on tightly to his seat as the Huey slammed into a hover and descended to LZ Mike. Their assignment: To cut the enemy infiltration routes in the areas northeast of Biên Hòa and the fire support base a few klicks away.

He hopped out of the chopper with his M16 locked and loaded. Sweeping back and forth, he scanned the area over his rifle sights as the rest of the men piled out, taking up defensive positions around him. Sweat soaked his OD green cotton jungle fatigues. Mud covered his boots up to the shank. His heart beat like a trip hammer on overdrive in his chest.

The sky looked like a dark, angry swarm of green wasps with all the choppers in the air. The "Sky-Troopers" of the 2nd Platoon, led by Captain Jefferson, came into LZ Mike behind Chris' 1st Platoon, 1st Battalion. The combined, overlapping rotor wash flattened the three-foot-tall yellowish-green cogon grass in circular, wavy patterns. The fluffy, white, plume-like seed heads flew everywhere like swirling snow.

The crappy Vietnam weather with a ceiling lower than 500 feet and visibility less than a mile and a half delayed their initial planned insertion at 0700 hours.

Designated air cover consisting of a pair of Air Force fighters flew around the area on standby. The same with the 155mm towed Howitzers of Alpha Battery, 1st Battalion, 30th Artillery.

A B-52 Arc Light strike yesterday removed the nearby tree cover leaving smoldering splintered trunks. The bomb craters appeared as orange, oozing lesions in the hillsides. Only the underbrush of tall elephant grass thick enough to hide animals or humans remained.

Intelligence said the NVA and Viet Cong had stashes of food, small arms, ammunition, rockets, mortars, and recoilless rifle rounds. It was good the American forces controlled the air with fighters, bombers, and helicopters.

Chris waved his men to follow him then adjusted his helmet from his eyes as the 2nd Platoon took off in the opposite direction of their target.

The plan, trap the NVA troops in their tunnels and hooches and squeeze the supply line dry.

As the 1st Platoon spread out, Chris took point, a position not normally taken by the ranking officer. The newest guy usually walked point. Today was different. His choice. He moved forward slowly and cautiously, watching for any signs of hidden booby traps. While most wouldn't kill you, they could make your life a living hell while recovering at a field hospital and take away your ability to have children. For him, that last part was out anyway unless a miracle happened with his wife.

They entered a nearby village so small it didn't have a name on the map but a number—05. Smoke rose from the cooking fires with bamboo A-frames and iron pots scattered around the small compound.

A water buffalo was tied to a pole by its nose ring. Chickens ran around scratching at the dirt, searching for a bug to eat. A few thin, mangy, almost hairless dogs wagging their tails approached wanting food then scurried off when they didn't get any.

His men were well-trained and knew what to do. Two troopers peeled off from the column into the first hut. Nothing but bamboo supports covered with woven rattan walls, a thatched grass roof, and a dirt floor. Simplicity at its best for the poor peasants who lived there.

The next two men up did the same with the second hut. Quickly they cleared the small village of ten hunts, two sheds full of farming tools, and a corral with one old gray swaybacked horse in it.

As each two-man team reappeared from a structure or corner, they herded the villagers in the local garb of brown homespun cotton shirts, pants, and floppy straw hats, ahead of them. The men used their rifle muzzles as an incentive for them to keep moving forward in groups of one, two, and a few threes. In total, they found twenty men and women but no children. Which seemed strange. They sat the village residents around the water well's stacked limestone wall for easy containment.

To Chris, this seemed too easy. With as much firepower rumored to be in this village, he'd thought the VC sympathizers would have put up a fight.

As his men continued to search the camp, Chris leaned against the wall of a hut to observe everything going on around him. One Vietnamese man in his early twenties kept looking down the well then back at the American soldiers as they roamed around the village.

Chris motioned at two of the men watching the prisoners. "Move the villagers over to the corral and keep a close eye on them." Chris thought for a moment. "Better yet, search them again and tie them up for our safety."

"Yes, sir," the men replied, using their rifle muzzles as cattle prods to push the villagers over to the corral.

Yanking his flashlight off the shoulder strap of his web gear, Chris shined it into the well and caught the odor of something besides water. "Did anyone stick this well with something to determine the depth?"

"No, sir," Corporal Nunez said, slinging his M16.

"Someone get a pole and stick this well."

Nunez took off.

Chris stuck his head down into the well. It looked deep and dark. He smelled gasoline or some kind of chemical, but it shouldn't be in drinking water. Since Nunez was taking too long, Chris lowered the bucket hung on the pulley bracket to the water. He let it drop to the bottom. The rope only went down six feet. It wasn't that deep at all. And that wasn't enough water for twenty people and the animals.

Nunez returned with a long fence pole. "Found something, Major."

"Perfect." Chris pointed at the water. "Break out whatever's in there. I don't want to use rifles until we're sure it won't blow up and us with it."

Nunez started pounding. At his tenth strike, a loud wet thwack sounded, large bubbles appeared, and the water disappeared into the hole. With a wooden plank floor in view, Nunez stuck the end of the pole into the hole and started to use it as a lever, pushing down with his full weight on both hands.

"Wait a minute." Chris waved over several men and pointed at the hole. "If there's someone down there, use him...or her for target practice." He pulled a grenade from his web belt and got ready to chuck it into the hole if needed. "Now, Nunez."

Nunez used the bar as a lever. The wood cracked. One plank broke out then another. The men leaned closer with their fingers on their M16 triggers. With each break, Nunez pushed the wood pieces aside.

Chris shined his flashlight down the hole with his free hand at two wet male faces and AK-47s pointed at him and his men. He backed up as his men unleashed hell's fury into the well with their M16s. Empty brass casings bounced around at their feet. The sound was deafening coming from the hole. Smoke wisped from their M16 barrels when they stopped firing and reloaded with full magazines.

He leaned over to look, sure that no one was alive. The well's stone walls were coated with blood and grayish-white brain matter. Two bodies lay on top of several wooden crates.

"Do we get them out, Major?" Nunez asked.

"No. Too dangerous if there's a booby trap or two down there. Find something that burns and pour it down that stinking hole. Then pour a trail to it, and we'll stand back at the village edge, light the trail, and watch whatever's in that well burn. That way, if it explodes, we're clear. And we give those gooks the burial they deserve."

"And what do you put in the report about weapons?"

"We wait until the fire burns out, find out what's in there, and log it for the report. In the meantime, Katz, you, and Stoker turn the animals loose and run the villagers out of here. We're going to torch this VC nest so they can't use it again."

"Are you sure, sir?" Katz wondered out loud.

"Yes, I'm sure, Corporal. I know what you're thinking, and I sure as hell don't want to make these people homeless, but I can't leave this village intact. Those are our orders. As much as I'd like to disobey them, the next guy might not let those villagers live."

0900 Hours
June 3, 1969
1st Cavalry Division Headquarters
Phước Vĩnh, South Vietnam
III Corps

Reading through his after-action report about Biên Hòa Province one more time, Chris affixed his signature at the bottom. He flipped to the appendix page and checked the numbers on what was found in village 05. At least what they managed to confirm in the burned-out well through melted receivers, barrels, bullet casings, mortar rounds, a few semi-charred intact wooden boxes, and ammo cans.

Viet Cong KIA – 2
Village 05 destroyed
No civilian casualties
No US Army casualties

Weapons found and destroyed:
10,000 AK-47 rounds
5,000 heavy machine gun rounds
40 mortar rounds
22 anti-personnel mines

100 pounds of explosives
10 Type 97 hand grenades
20 AK-47 rifles
10 SKS rifles
1 Sturmgewehr 44 rifle
1 Type 92 heavy machine gun
1 Bren light machine gun

Miscellaneous destroyed:
200 pounds of rations (rice, corn, salt)

Chris signed the bottom of this page, signifying he reviewed it as accurate. They probably destroyed more. But that was all they could find.

CHAPTER 4

1500 Hours
June 15, 1969
1st Cavalry Division Headquarters
Phước Vĩnh, South Vietnam
III Corps

Bang-bang-bang. Someone was knocking on his office door. Only Captain Jefferson was that heavy-handed. It might come from his Golden Gloves boxer days as a light heavyweight.

After opening his eyes and straightening in his chair, finally hearing the rock music coming from the radio set to the American Forces Vietnam Network, Chris called out, "Enter."

He must have fallen asleep after returning from the mess hall. Oops. Not a great example to set for his men with Charlie in camp among the "vetted" locals. It was a good thing no one saw him. At least his rifle was close, locked and loaded.

Captain Jefferson entered the office with a large box in his hands. "You missed mail call, sir. Thought you'd want this." He set the box on the desk.

Chris looked at the return address – Kara Patterson, Ft. Hood, TX. "Thanks, Captain. You're dismissed. I don't want any visitors." He waited until Jefferson closed the door before opening the box.

On top of a piece of cardboard lay a standard white envelope. He picked it up and took a deep whiff. It smelled of her favorite perfume - Chanel No. 5. Laying the envelope aside, he pulled off the cardboard.

Inside the box were pre-packaged cookies, beef jerky, crackers, peanut butter, candy bars, gum, Twinkies, Ding Dongs, and hard candy. Staples hard to come by in Vietnam. Under the food were clear plastic packages of new underwear, t-shirts, boot socks, razors, and the best thing of all, a large package of soft toilet paper. One-ply Army toilet paper felt like sixty grit sandpaper on a good day and even worse with a regular bout of dysentery.

He'd take everything to his quarters when he got off duty in a couple of hours and leaned back in his chair. Again, he smelled the envelope, imagining his wife's face, the feeling of her silky hair, and the soft skin of every part of her body. He wanted to make love to her. To touch her. Feel her breath on his neck. Caress her. Kiss her.

He carefully slit the envelope open with his pocket knife to keep from marring her handwriting and pulled out the letter. It smelled even stronger of Chanel No. 5 like she'd sprayed it directly on the paper. He missed her so much.

My dear Chris,

I hope a smile appears on your face and your eyes light up as you read this letter. My heart aches at what you are facing in Vietnam. I see the battles on the news and my concern grows with each newscast. I'm scared for you. My heart cringes at what could happen. I know I married the Army when I married you and I accepted being an Army wife and all the responsibilities that brings. Being an Army officer was your dream. Your calling. What I didn't know was how lonely I would be.

They finally set Amanda's headstone last week. The funeral home kept apologizing for the delay, but they had to take care of the soldiers' stones first. I started painting to keep my mind occupied and joined the women's auxiliary here on base to help out.

I stay strong for you. For us. For our departed Amanda. Your courage keeps me going, running through me with each memory of you. I keep your picture close to my heart in the locket you gave me as an early anniversary gift before your deployment.

I think about you every day and all our wonderful experiences together. That day at Waikiki Beach when you built that lopsided sandcastle. Our first official date at that fancy French restaurant, and you ordered Escargot in butter without knowing they're snails. I'll never forget the disgusted look on your face. Us riding that big wooden roller coaster at Six Flags when you raised your hands in the air and screamed at the top of the big hill. I cherish those memories.

Not even Vietnam can break the chain that wraps our hearts together. Not even death can make that happen. Don't focus on us being apart. Focus on us being together again one day.

I want to feel the heat of your skin next to me. Inside me. We will be reunited when God and the Army finally send you home to me. I hope you return to me whole, unchanged, unhurt, and unscarred while maintaining the courage I admire with every fiber of my being.

Keep smiling your beautiful smile and don't be sad. You are always in my thoughts as I know I am in yours. Enjoy all the goodies I packed for you. I miss you terribly. Don't ever forget how much I love you.

With all my love,

Kara Patterson

Chris traced the outline of her lips in red lipstick under her signature, seeing every line that made up those luscious, tender entrances to her mouth. He placed it to his lips, holding her picture from his pocket against his chest. A tear rolled down his cheek as he thought about kissing her and smelling her perfume in person.

Carefully, he returned the letter to the envelope and placed it and her picture on his end table next to his loaded Colt M1911A1 .45 caliber pistol. A hazard of war where the enemy could be anyone. "Vetted" locals could enter without notice to kill you.

At this moment, he wanted to go home to be with her. To see his daughter's headstone in person. But he took an oath long before he met Kara. This was his job. He was a soldier. An officer. His dream as she said. His career. He had to finish it. But it sure was hard.

CHAPTER 5

0900 Hours
July 26, 1969
Bình Phước Province, South Vietnam
III Corps

As the lead truck rattled along about eighteen klicks south of An Lộc, Chris kept an ever-watchful eye out for enemy activity in the tall grass and deep ditches beside the dirt road that resembled a bumpy goat path. Most of the thick canopy of trees had been thinned back by bombing and chemical spraying. He'd seen rows of the orange-striped fifty-five-gallon barrels near the base airstrip.

The passenger side gave him a great view of the front and sides of the vehicle. All he saw so far was waving cogon and elephant grass. Beside him in the seat, his M16 was loaded, charged, and ready to rock if something happened. And in this area, it usually did.

His 1st Platoon had been tasked with security for a convoy of towed 105 and 155mm Howitzers to help fortify Firebase Thunder III, manned by the 2nd Battalion, 2nd Mechanized Infantry.

Tired of nothing but paperwork for the last month, he decided to join them. He hated being still. That is not what he signed on for when he joined the Army, fought in Korea, and went to West Point, branching Infantry, not Quartermaster.

Suddenly, a fiery explosion went off in front of the truck, peppering the hood and spidering the windshield with shrapnel. The driver applied the brakes to stop.

"No," Chris yelled, grabbing his M16 and pointing it out the open window. "That's an RPG. We don't want to be sitting ducks stopped in the road. Speed the fuck up."

The engine revved as the driver, Sergeant Levy, a young man from Brooklyn, pressed the accelerator. Machine gun and rocket-propelled grenade fire opened up on them from both sides. The Browning .50 cal gunners on both sides of the truck bed swept their weapons across a fifty-yard-wide path as they bounced along the road, leaving chopped grass and chewed mud in their wake.

More than likely, whoever shot the RPG at them was out of range for their small arms, but they continued firing. Good thing he loaded the trucks down with sandbags, ammo, and scrounged iron plates, and he insisted the men wear their heavy flak jackets, even in the oppressive heat and humidity.

The sporadic RPG fire turned into thicker machine gun fire closer to the road. Chris could tell they were targeting his truck to block the convoy's path and put all of his men in a shooting gallery with the only way out through the gauntlet of RPGs. He wondered if he just screwed up by continuing. No, Firebase Thunder needed the artillery, and it was their job to get it there. Now he knew why and wished he'd managed to score a few APCs for this mission. But The First Team didn't stop, didn't quit, no matter the odds. The brotherhood of blood.

Chris heard a bullet whiz by his ear through the window. The truck started slowing down. He turned to the driver to tell him to keep going, but the words stopped in his throat. Levy was slumped back in his seat, a hole in his right side and blood soaking his green fatigues.

He wedged his M16 into the center of the dash and pulled Levy over him as he scooted under into the driver's seat. The one thing he could tell. Levy was still breathing, therefore alive. With that amount of blood loss, the young sergeant wouldn't be for long.

Jamming his foot into the accelerator, Chris gripped the wheel with his sweaty hands. They couldn't be far from Firebase Thunder III. The minutes seemed like hours.

As they topped a small hill, he saw the walls of the firebase with the gate open. Chris drove the truck inside the gate, pulled off to the side, and slammed on the brakes. He leaned over to check Levy's pulse. It was thready and weak, but there.

"Medic, medic," he screamed out the window, pressing a bandage from his web gear over the bleeding wound.

The passenger side door opened, and a soldier stuck his head into the cab. He nodded at Chris then pulled Levy out.

Chris jumped out of the driver's side and ran around the truck, dropping down on one knee close to where the medic worked on Levy.

Captain Jefferson ran up and knelt beside him. "Are you okay, sir?"

"Fine. Sit-rep," Chris ordered.

"All trucks and weapons accounted for. No dead. Five wounded." Jefferson pointed at Levy. Including Sergeant Levy. Dust off inbound. I called for one as we entered the gate."

"Good job, Captain. Have the men help the arty guys get these weapons unhitched and secured. Then they can get some chow, such as it is." He hated C-rats as much as the next man. But as long as he didn't get beans and motherfuckers, he'd be satisfied. The spaghetti and chicken weren't bad, covered with a lot of Tabasco sauce and ketchup.

Chris looked up at the chop of incoming rotors. A Huey with a red cross painted on the nose was landing across the compound. He followed the two men carrying Levy on the stretcher to the idling chopper. Within moments, all the wounded were onboarded, and the chopper lifted off. Each second of time meant life or death.

The medic that tended to Levy placed a hand on Chris' arm. "Are you hurt, sir?"

"Huh...no." Chris looked himself over. "That's Levy's blood. Where's that chopper headed?"

"Nha Trang." The medic pointed at Chris. "Why is there blood leaking from the hole in your shirt?"

Huh? Chris checked himself again. Then he saw the bleeding gash on his left shoulder. It didn't hurt. "Oh, I guess I was hit." Not even worth reporting.

The medic probed the wound. "Looks like a deep bullet graze. I'll bandage it up. Just see the doc when you get back to the base. You might need a tetanus shot. Out here, you don't want this getting infected."

"You got that right." Chris wondered if that same bullet hit Levy. He only remembered the one coming into the truck cab. That didn't mean there couldn't have been more. His arm started hurting as the adrenaline wore off. Maybe he would get checked by a doctor when he got back to base. He didn't want to get put out of action for something so insignificant.

CHAPTER 6

1300 Hours
July 30, 1969
5th Special Forces Base
Nha Trang, South Vietnam
II Corps

After checking on his men at the hospital, Chris parked his jeep at the 5th Special Forces headquarters building and went inside to the front desk. "Is Lieutenant Colonel MacKenzie in his office," he asked the clerk.

"He went to the mess hall thirty minutes ago, sir," the sergeant said.

Hope their chow is better than ours. "Thanks." Chris exited the building and followed the signs.

He stopped on the walkway to watch three MPs dragging a large man, at least six-foot-two and nearly two-hundred-and-fifty pounds with Native American features, toward what he assumed by the barred windows was the base stockade. *Wonder what he did?*

Once they disappeared into the building, Chris continued to the mess hall. He pushed through the swinging double doors and looked for his friend. Sitting at one of the long tables in the center of the room was Jackson with his back to him and Major Harry Russell. They looked as if they were in a heated conversation about something the way both men were talking with their hands. It reminded him of when he spent six months in Italy at Camp Darby. Italians have a hand gesture for everything.

Chris made his way to the table and stood behind Jackson, looking down at his dark blond high and tight hair.

Harry had a slight smile.

"Mind if I join you?" Chris asked.

Jackson turned, holding a large white bag of frozen peas to his left eye and gazing up at Chris. "Sure, what brings you to our neck of the woods, Major?"

He had to rub it in that he's now my superior officer. I'll catch up soon. "Never mind that." Chris sat next to Jackson. "What happened to you?"

"Broke up a fight. Got hit with a right cross." Jackson lowered the bag for a moment then put it back. He had one hell of a swollen black and blue shiner.

"Would the guy I saw being dragged down the street have been part of that fight?"

"Big guy with a shitty attitude?" Harry asked, running a hand through his brown flat-top hair.

"If you mean it took three MPs his size to get him to the stockade, yes." Chris liked Harry Russell. He matched up with Jackson perfectly and not just in height, weight, and personalities that meshed seamlessly. The man had a sense of humor to go along with excellent leadership skills, bravery, and discipline. Too bad he went to ROTC instead of West Point, or he'd be a Lt. Colonel by now. Still, Chris saw him having his own command one day.

"That's him. Sergeant First Class Dakota Blackwater."

"Blackwater? Even I've heard about him. The man loves to start drunken bar fights. Six months ago, he put three guys from the 1st Cav in the hospital at Cam Ranh Bay and caused over a thousand dollars in damage to Gunslingers. The judge ordered him to make restitution and busted him to Staff Sergeant. When did he get his rank back?"

"Last week." Harry tapped the table. "Today he wasn't drunk. He disagreed with another motor pool grease monkey on the reassembly of a deuce and a half engine. Don't ask me why. That's all I know. The other guy wouldn't give us the whole story. I'm betting it was more than just about a truck. I heard someone whisper the other guy called him…" He glanced around and lowered his voice. "A no-good blanket-assed injun."

"Ouch. It's still not a reason to fight. What are you going to do with him?" Chris asked, looking over at Jackson and wincing. That eye had to hurt.

Jackson drew a deep breath. "Transfer him from the motor pool."

"To where?" Harry asked.

"Your command under Captain Mason. He needs a heavy weapons specialist to replace Bowers."

"What!" Harry exclaimed. "I don't want that mother fucking troublemaker."

"He does have a point, JJ." Chris pointed at Jackson's frozen pea bag-covered eye.

"And a really good one," Jackson said. "I agree he's a troublemaker and should be court-martialed for striking an officer. I still may do it depending on his attitude when I go talk to him after he cools off. But I believe he can be turned around. Blackwater was at the top of his class in basic and jump school. The same with Special Forces training. When he's focused, he is an excellent soldier, brave to a fault with great instincts in combat. His last CO recommended him for the Silver Star for saving five men in an ambush. I don't want to send a good man to prison for doing something stupid because someone insulted him. I walked into the punch. He wasn't aiming for me."

Harry shook his head. "He sure tried to go after you to hit you again when they dragged him out of here."

"True. He was mad about going to the stockade. He's looking at me from an enlisted point of view. To him, I'm just another stupid officer." Jackson pointed at Harry and Chris. "Like you two."

"And both of you know that because you were enlisted during the Korean War," Harry said.

Chris and Jackson looked at each other.

"Exactly," they said together.

Harry released an exasperated sigh. "So, I get the troublemaker and hope he doesn't pound me into the dirt with those ham-sized fists."

"That's the plan," Jackson replied.

"Wonderful."

"Well, those are the decisions one has to make as the commanding officer of a big-time outfit like the 5th Special Forces," Chris said.

"Ha-ha. Funny. It's only temporary until General Abrams gets someone he trusts in here to replace me. One day..." Jackson paused. "When you finally make rank, this'll be you."

"I sure hope so." Chris couldn't hold himself back. "As much as I'd like to stick around to see how your little experiment with Blackwater plays out, I've got to get back to my base."

Before Chris could stand, Jackson grabbed his arm. "You never told me why you're here?"

"Visiting three of my men in the hospital. Got zapped on a convoy mission a few days ago."

"Heard about it. Did you get hit? You keep scratching your left shoulder."

Chris touched the bandage under his shirt. He didn't realize what he was doing. "Minor graze that's healing well. Not worth the Purple Heart." He stood and gripped Jackson's shoulder. "Take care of yourself. I'll see you when I see you. Catch you on the flip side."

As he pushed the doors open to exit the building, he realized he had forgotten to tell Jackson about marrying Kara. Oh well, he'd tell him another time. He didn't want Jackson making a big deal out of him being wounded. It really was minor.

CHAPTER 7

1900 Hours
August 28, 1969
1st Cavalry Division Officers Quarters
Phước Vĩnh, South Vietnam
III Corps

As Chris packed his duffle bag for a week's leave in Hawaii with his wife, he heard running footsteps in the hall outside his room. Then came the sound of rapid, heavy knocking on his door. Did something important come up? Was his leave canceled? He wanted to see his wife.

With slow feet and a lot of reluctance, he answered the door. Standing there was a huffing Captain Jefferson with a folded piece of paper in his outstretched right hand.

"Major, this just came over the wire. I thought you'd want to see it right away, sir," Jefferson said.

Did something happen to Kara? Did her plane crash? Chris took the note. "Thanks, Captain." He closed and locked the door then sat on his bunk. With shaky hands, he unfolded the paper, unsure of what he was about to read.

To: Major General Ryan Holcomb
Commanding Officer, 1st Special Forces
Fort Bragg, NC

From: Major Carsen Paccione
Temporary commanding officer, 5th Special Forces Group
Nha Trang, South Vietnam

Subject: Members of ODA-312, C Company, 2nd Battalion, 5th
Special Forces Group
Missing in Action

On 26 August 1969, ODA-312 went on a search-and-destroy mission in support of the 101st Airborne Division. Before arrival at the LZ, a distress call was dispatched for two downed

20

Navy F-4s in the Central Highlands of the II Corps in an area of heavy enemy activity.

Lt. Colonel J.J. MacKenzie, temporary commanding officer of the 5th Special Forces Group, was in command of the mission. Close to the location of the downed Naval Aviators and no pararescue available, Lt. Colonel MacKenzie attempted a rescue.

The last communication with UH-1H, S/N 10-777, tail number 68-16118, call sign Hercules, was that it was struck in the tail rotor by an RPG. At this point, all communication was lost with the aircraft. An overflight of the location located a burned UH-1 helicopter. The concurrent insertion of a pararescue team yielded seven identified bodies, including two Naval Aviators.

KIA are as follows:
5th Special Forces
Sergeant Samuel B. Thompson (Found with aircraft)
Sergeant Hector M. Ruiz (Found with aircraft)
Sergeant Brian B. Henderson (Found with aircraft)
Sergeant Herman J. Chomosh (Found with aircraft)

281st Assault Helicopter Company:
Staff Sergeant Kyle N. Warden (Found with aircraft)

United States Navy:
Lieutenant Jacob Holloway (Found with gunshot wound to the head)
Lieutenant Richard Marion (Found with gunshot wound to the head)

Missing in Action are as follows:
Lt. Colonel Jackson J. MacKenzie – 5th SFG
Major Harrison A. Russell – 5th SFG
Captain William L. Mason – 5th SFG
Captain Francis K. Nelson – 281st AHC
1st Lieutenant Tyler M. Carter – 5th SFG
Sergeant First Class Dakota C. Blackwater – 5th SFG
Staff Sergeant Michael P. Roberts – 5th SFG

Chris stared at the words. His oldest friend was listed missing in action. "Ahh fuck! JJ. Geez." He pulled his dog tag chain from under his t-shirt. On an extra loop of ball chain hung a small silver cross and a St. Michael's medal engraved with his name. Christmas gifts from Jackson their last year at West Point.

"What in the hell happened?" He slammed his hand against the wall. How would he tell Kara her childhood friend from USMC Camp Pendleton in San Diego was missing, maybe dead or a POW? That was even worse.

He cringed at that grim thought. Like all American military personnel in Southeast Asia, he'd heard about the cruelty of the North Vietnamese to American prisoners and seen the propaganda leaflets. They didn't follow the Geneva Convention. To them, the men weren't prisoners but war criminals. Therefore, they were subject to starvation and torture. Fate could be ruthless sometimes.

August 29, 1969
Oahu Hilton – Rainbow Tower
14th Floor
Honolulu, Hawaii

Slowly turning the key in the lock, Chris heard the click that unlocked the door. He needed a long, hot shower. His summer khaki uniform was wrinkled, sweaty, and reeked of body odor. It had been a long commercial flight to Hawaii on a Pan Am 707 with already drunk young soldiers fresh from a combat zone. They were ready for a week of good times at Fort Derussy, an R&R facility on Waikiki Beach. He made other plans, wanting alone time, not a crowd.

The soldiers, mostly privates, ignored the gold oak leaf on his collar, and military courtesy went out the window. They blatantly hit on the pretty and curvy female flight attendants in front of him. Not that he blamed them after six months in the bush. It was a way to let off steam. He might have, too, if he wasn't married.

The room had a long glass window with a sliding door and a balcony. They would have a panoramic view of the Pacific Ocean and the waves lapping on the sand against a royal blue sky. The best part, a private bathroom with a sink, bathtub, soft terry cloth towels, and a working toilet. Not a stinky latrine made of a wooden building with splinter-filled toilet seats over a waste-filled hole with dive-bombing biting black flies as big as your hand. He'd have to curb his mouth. A nasty habit that returned from being back in a war zone. Kara didn't like him to curse around her.

He threw his duffle bag on the bed and removed the sweet-smelling colorful lai from his neck given to him by greeters at the terminal. As he stripped off his shirt and t-shirt, he heard the lock click.

He turned. The door swung open, and there stood Kara, wearing a light blue summer dress with her hair in a ponytail. A smile stretched across her face, and her eyes twinkled. She dropped her suitcase, shut the door, and ran into his outstretched arms.

Chris buried his face into her hair, enjoying the freshly laundered scent he missed so much. He kissed her, enjoying every moment of her luscious red lips. This was heaven. Slowly, he guided her to the bed and sat beside her, running his fingers through her hair. He couldn't get enough of her.

Kara caught his hand. "What's wrong, Chris?"

She read him so well. "What makes you think something's wrong? I'm just happy to see you."

"Then you'd be babbling your head off. What's wrong?"

Chris pulled the somewhat damp, worn, folded report from his shirt pocket and handed it to her. "This."

She unfolded the paper and put a hand over her mouth. "Oh my God. Any more news?"

Chris shook his head. "No. All we can do is hope."

"Because it's a hazard of war, right?" Kara said disgustedly.

"Yes." He didn't know another answer and placed a hand on hers. "Should I call his wife?"

"Given you only know what's on that piece of paper, probably not. The Army may know something you don't. You don't want to jump the gun with the worst."

"True." Chris wished there was something he could do. But right now, Kara was right as always.

"All we can do is pray and hope for the best." She placed a hand on his sweaty bare chest. "Since you've already started undressing, keep going."

"Yes, ma'am," he replied gently, tossing his bag on the floor.

Kara removed her dress, bra, and underwear and lay on the bed, smiling up at him.

He stripped off the rest of his clothes, closed the blinds, and climbed into bed next to her. He'd take a shower…later.

The weather in Honolulu was perfect. The sun shone brightly like a radiant yellow-orange diamond every day. On the first day, they swam in the cerulean blue water of Waikiki Beach until they looked like prunes. The sand was warm and inviting as they slept holding hands under a cabana in lounge chairs and walked on the wet sand until the shadows grew long.

They ate dinner in every nice restaurant within walking distance of the hotel. Chris knew he'd pay for that by the end of the week. His gut would rebel about the rich food instead of mess hall fare, and he'd wind up constipated. Sometimes hard was worse than soft and liquid.

He rented a small convertible, and they drove to the North Shore with the wind in their hair to watch the surfers. Kara wanted him to try. Chris said no. He didn't want to look like a fool when he fell off the board and got eaten by sharks. That would look bad on his final eval. Decision-making – zero.

They shopped at the Hilton Hawaiian Village, went horseback riding in the hills, and ate fresh-picked pineapple at the Dole Plantation.

On the last night, they attended a luau. Kara joined the girls hula dancing on stage in a grass skirt as Chris took photos for her album. She was a natural. At least, he thought so.

When they uncovered the pig from the imu, a traditional Hawaiian underground oven made of hot lava rocks, the smell made Chris' mouth water. Unlike the other food he remembered buried in the ground during the Korean War, kimchi – fermented cabbage. That stuff buried all over the country made him want to puke.

CHAPTER 8

0255 Hours
November 20, 1970
1st Cavalry Division Officers Quarters
Phước Vĩnh, South Vietnam

Explosions went up on both sides of the road, bringing their convoy to a halt. Chris piled out of the second jeep, taking cover beside it near the front wheel well. He looked to his right, nodding at Lt. Colonel Jackson MacKenzie, who nodded back. Jackson eased himself around the front of his jeep with a grenade in his right hand and pulled the pin.

As Jackson leaned back to throw, a round struck him in the right shoulder. He fell hard to his knees but managed to launch the grenade several yards past the brush-filled ditch on the other side of the road, where muzzle flashes erupted with abandon.

An explosion went up, sending mud twenty-five feet into the air, causing everyone to duck. Rifle launched grenades landed around them. Shrapnel flew outward and upward, piercing the air over their heads in all directions. Bullets impacted the ground everywhere.

"Medic!" Chris yelled, making his way in a crouch to the front of Jackson's jeep. He inched around with his rifle pointed at the enemy and released a full-auto burst to clear the area. Then he looked down to grab Jackson by his web gear shoulder straps to pull him to safety. Jackson wasn't there. A wide blood trail led off into the ditch on the other side of the road.

Chris leveled his M16 over the jeep hood and scanned the area to find where that trail went. He followed it as blood dripped off the waist-high grass. Fifty feet away, he saw two Viet Cong sappers dressed in black dragging a blood-covered Jackson into the fog-shrouded tree line near the creek.

Jackson fought them, trying to wrench himself free. He bit the arm of one captor, using that split-second diversion to pull his KA-BAR combat knife from the sheath. Another sapper yanked it from his grasp, placing the blade against Jackson's throat.

Chris couldn't fire, afraid that he'd hit Jackson. And he couldn't move, his body locked in that position. He watched the fog swirl as Jackson and

25

his captors disappeared into the mist. His muscles wouldn't answer his commands to chase after them to save his friend.

He heard Jackson screaming, "Chris, help me," over and over until it faded into nothing. The shelling and gunfire stopped. The air stilled. Only the jungle sounds remained – frogs, crickets, an occasional monkey calling out, and in the distance, the roar of a tiger.

Chris opened his eyes. Moonlight streamed through an open window, illuminating the room. Instead of a muddy road, he lay in his bunk wearing boxer shorts. He kicked off his blanket and sat up, knocking over his jungle boots on the floor. Confused, he looked around.

On the small table beside his bed, Kara's picture. His M1967 combat web gear with belt, suspenders, two ammo pouches, first aid kit, two canteens, buttpack, combat knife, and holstered Colt M1911A1 .45 caliber pistol hung on a chair over a fatigue shirt. A loaded M16 was propped in a corner. Above his bunk, a helmet dangled from a long nail.

Why did he dream about Jackson? And the events of the dream didn't happen. They never served in the same unit in Vietnam. Sighing, he checked the wall clock. 0300 hours. Since he couldn't sleep, he dressed in his fatigues and boots, put on his web gear, grabbed his M16, then headed to headquarters. He needed some air. He'd grab a cup of coffee while checking the incoming dispatches.

As he crossed the compound, the illuminated window of the base chapel caught his eye. He changed direction and headed there. While he didn't want to discuss his dream with anyone who could report it to his CO, a priest wasn't obligated to pass something told in confidence up the chain of command. Maybe he could make sense of the dream.

Chris slung his M16 then went inside the bamboo-walled, grass-roofed rectangular building and stopped. It looked like any other chapel he'd seen. Wooden pews on both sides with a center aisle. In the front of the room, the altar - a five-foot wooden cross on a pedestal behind the sacrificial table. Off to the side sat a lectern.

This was the first time he'd stepped foot in a church since his daughter's funeral. He didn't see a point. God took away his little girl, not even a minute old. That day, he lost most of his faith.

He walked slowly up the center aisle, checking for anyone kneeling in the pews. The Viet Cong could be that devious. He didn't want to be shot in the back. The secondary reason - he didn't want anyone to know he came to see the priest before working hours. They might ask questions he didn't want to answer.

At the altar, he knelt, said a silent prayer, crossed himself, and stood.

26

"To what do I own the pleasure, my son?" said a male voice behind him.

Chris spun around, simultaneously dropping his M16 into a ready position. "Where'd you come from?"

The Caucasian man, wearing green fatigues with captain's bars on one collar and a cross on the other, raised his hands. He had a silver cross and dog tags on a chain around his neck. "Easy, Major."

"Sorry, Father." Chris shouldered his M16. "You can never be too careful."

"True." He said, slowly lowering his hands. "I'm Father Moskovitz."

"Moskovitz? Isn't that a Jewish name?"

"Yes." The priest smiled. "My family converted in the 1880s to Catholicism. Why are you here, Major?"

"Patterson." Chris nodded at the back of the chapel. "Is there a place we can talk in private?"

Moskovitz pointed at a small ornate wooden cabinet with two doors against the wall. "Are you here for confession?"

Chris shook his head. "No."

"Oh, that kind of private. Follow me." Moskovitz headed toward the altar. He opened a door hidden by the cross, held it open for Chris then followed him inside.

"This is your inner sanctum, Father?" Chris looked around. The small room held one straight-backed wooden chair, a bunk with a standard Army-issued green wool blanket and a desk with a cross nailed to the wall over it. Open on the bunk, a black-bound Bible.

Father Moskovitz sat next to the Bible and motioned at a chair. "Please sit."

Chris sat, laying his M16 on the floor beside him.

"I'll ask again. To what do I owe the pleasure of your company at O dark thirty?"

"Bad dream."

"And you want to talk about it?"

Chris drew circles on the floor with his boot. "Yeah, I guess."

"If it were 'I guess,' you wouldn't be here," Moskovitz said, fingering his cross.

The priest was right. "Uh-huh."

"Something that happened to you on patrol?"

"No. It never happened." Chris told him about the dream.

"Who is this MacKenzie fellow to you?" Moskovitz asked.

"My oldest friend and West Point roommate," Chris replied.

"Have you called to check on him? It might help you get some sleep."

Chris ran his hand through his hair. "I can't. He's been MIA since August."

"Ahhh. There may be your problem. He's one of so many who've rolled past you on the bloody assembly line of this war."

"But why this time?" Chris asked. "I've seen men die. I've never dreamed of anyone being captured or killed before tonight."

"Instead of a replacement you just met yesterday, he's a friend, a confidant...a brother. Someone you've spent countless hours with pursuing the same dream."

"That still doesn't answer my question."

Moskovitz tapped the side of his head. "Dreaming is escapism for our minds. But after what happened to your friend, the war took the lead and invaded your dream. It made something normally peaceful a part of your—" Moskovitz pointed at the M16. "Reality. And you wake up screaming."

"I didn't tell you I woke up screaming."

"You didn't?" Moskovitz smiled. "Okay, that's rhetorical. But you did...in your heart. Or you wouldn't be here."

Chris nodded. "True. Will I keep dreaming about him?"

"That's up to you and God."

"What can I do about it?"

"You came to me. I have only one suggestion."

"Pray?"

"Can you think of anything better?" Moskovitz tossed a folded OD-green Army towel on the floor in front of Chris.

"What's that for?"

"Your knees. The floor is full of splinters and broken-off rusty nails. Unless you enjoy pain and want a trip to the infirmary for a tetanus shot."

"No thanks." Chris knelt on the towel as Moskovitz did the same on a similar towel beside him.

They bowed their heads and recited the Lord's Prayer together. It wasn't much. But at least it helped his spirit and maybe his friend, wherever he might be.

1800 Hours
December 25, 1969
1st Cavalry Division Mess Hall
Phước Vĩnh, South Vietnam
III Corps

Going through the mess hall buffet line, Chris got his Christmas meal. The food looked like dog food. Spam shaped like something between a football, duck, chicken, and a turkey. Spamducken, the server called it. Chris wasn't sure what it was supposed to be. The Hawaiians might love the salty ham-colored stuff, but he hated it. The server even sliced a piece off as if it was real.

The semi-stiff off-colored mashed potatoes resembled wallpaper paste. They were covered in lumpy brown gravy with black specks that might be pepper or fly casings. The yeast roll bounced off the plate onto his nasty stained plastic tray. Overcooked mushy green beans and carrots rounded out the meal. For dessert, bright-orange colored pumpkin-flavored runny pie in an overdone crust covered by yellowed whipped cream.

Around him, tinny Christmas music played through rusted speakers bolted to the ceiling. On one long mess table in the center of the room sat a scraggly pine tree cut down in the nearby jungle. Handmade and commercial ornaments hung from thin wire on its branches. A frayed gold rope garland encircled the tree with silver tinsel thrown haphazardly in large clumps over it. On top, a star constructed of a piece of sheet metal and covered with red glitter. Underneath the tree were rolls of one-ply toilet paper with twine bows on top.

Chris took his meal back to his quarters in the officers' barracks and sat on his bunk with his tray. He turned on his radio to hear Christmas music from the Armed Forces Vietnam Network and placed Kara's picture in front of him. That way, he could eat with her. He missed her so much. While better than C-rations, the food tasted like it looked – crap.

On his end table sat his Christmas tree. A small pine tree in a clay pot he bought in Saigon. At least it was alive, not dead. Whether he could keep it alive was another matter. He had a brown thumb. When he was in the field, no one would water it. He wrapped a thin red ribbon he found in the trash around the tree. As a star, he pinned one of his gold oak leaves on top.

After eating what he could, Chris set the tray on the floor. He'd feed the stray dog outside the building later. He pulled a wrapped box from under his bunk. It came in last week's care package of treats, cookies, and toilet paper from Kara. The note said, "Do not open until Christmas."

Carefully, he removed the beautiful red bow and green paper one fold at a time. He used his pocket knife to slit the tape securing the top flaps of the box. Inside was a pink teddy bear wearing an Army OD-green jungle uniform and plastic black combat boots with miniature dog tags and a name tag on the shirt – Amanda.

Chris took it out and clutched it to his chest. He sniffed, wiping a sleeve across his eyes, then placed the bear gently on his pillow. If someone commented about the pink bear, he'd laugh it off, snarl, then give them KP duty. Peeling potatoes in the mess hall under the stern gaze of a hardened mess sergeant for a weekend should teach them not to laugh.

CHAPTER 9

0800 Hours
April 28, 1970
1st Cavalry Division Headquarters
Phước Vĩnh, South Vietnam

Colonel Best unfolded a map and spread it across the table in the conference room. "Everyone gather around."

Chris leaned across the table with the other battalion commanders to see the map more closely.

"On May 1st, you'll insert across the Cambodian border by helicopter here with the 3rd Brigade as part of Task Force Shoemaker." The colonel tapped a spot on the map circled in black. "West of the area known as the Fishhook, near the towns of Mimot and Snoul. The 3rd ARVN Airborne Brigade will assault the area to the north to cut off any escape. The 11th Armored Cavalry Regiment is on the south and east. Once your men secure the area, you'll push forward. You'll get to demonstrate the mobile part of Airmobile."

Chris almost rolled his eyes. They'd already proven the concept years ago. "What is our objective, sir? And why are we going into Cambodia? Isn't it still a neutral country?"

"It is." The colonel smiled. "Where are their supply lines, Patterson? Where does the NVA and Cong run to so we won't catch them?"

"The Cambodian Border."

"Exactly. President Nixon believes that by…and this is a direct quote…'Giving the South Vietnamese an operation of their own would be a major boost to their morale as well as provide a practical demonstration of the success of Vietnamization."

"Vietnamization! We all know that's a fucking joke."

"Major Patterson, I'd secure your mouth and opinion before it gets you in trouble."

"Yes, sir." *It's still a joke*. He'd better keep his mouth shut.

"Our objective, as you asked, is COSVN. The enemy's central office running operations in South Vietnam. Intelligence thinks it's in Cambodia."

Chris almost burst out laughing. Intelligence was a misnomer when it came to the MI guys. Most of them couldn't find their ass with both hands. "What else, sir? That can't be the only thing."

The colonel pursed his lips in annoyance. "No, you'll continue to locate and destroy enemy weapon caches and provisions. Since you've already been doing fast, light operations, this is pretty much more of the same."

So says the guy sitting in his office behind concertina wire, armed guards, and sandbags while we do the leap-frogging and taking chances. Chris looked at the colonel's annoyed face and decided to keep his opinions to himself for the rest of the briefing. They shoot at us. We shoot back. It's simple. The one thing he didn't want to do is wind up MIA like his oldest friend. Especially in Cambodia. No bodies had ever been found, and nothing heard outside of propaganda channels by their intelligence agents. He hoped JJ and his men didn't wind up in the infamous "Hanoi Hilton." But he didn't want to wind up there, either.

0600 Hours
May 4, 1970
Operation Rock Crusher
The "Fishhook"
Cambodia

Instead of the heavy opposition that Chris expected at the beginning of the operation from the amount of U.S. and ARVN units pouring over the Cambodian border, they were met by scattered and sporadic contact. The NVA seemed ill-prepared for the onslaught unleashed upon them.

As elements of his battalion patrolled around in the "Fishhook" region, looking for this mythical North Vietnamese command bunker called COSVN, they had to remain wary of their surroundings.

Chris watched the orange sun peek over the eastern horizon as he took a drink from his canteen. His body felt like a wet sponge with his OD-green jungle fatigues soaked in the aftermath of last night's storm and the never-ending humidity. He would never dry out. By the evening, he'd be one huge, itchy rash.

Surrounding him and A Company in a clearing of waist-high cogon grass was a thick canopy of trees—pine, palms, brushwood, and bamboo. Underbrush obscured any view of the ground.

Anything could be hiding from them – humans weren't the only things hunting American soldiers. So were the tigers, leopards, bears, and saltwater crocodiles. Spiders. Every insect imaginable - two-foot-long venomous Vietnamese centipedes, bombarding flies, malaria-carrying mosquitoes, giant scorpions, and biting Weaver ants.

He always imagined worms as things you fished with, not as the blood-sucking slimy leeches you didn't want in your jock. "Wait-a-minute" vines could suspend you in the air, trussed up like a pig ready for slaughter. Then came the things that slithered. Reticulated pythons, kraits, king cobras, and bamboo pit vipers - the three-step snakes. You take three steps, and then you die. The thought made him shiver inside.

Captain Jefferson came up beside him. "C Company on the other side of the ridge reports no contact."

"Good." Chris returned his canteen to the pouch on his web belt.

Boom!

Smoke went up in the distance, then the bang and pressure as shells fell earthward.

The men of A Company hit the dirt around him.

Chris leveled his weapon downrange, wondering what they stumbled into, a patrol or an entire battalion of NVA. He hoped it was just a patrol.

The shells rained closer as the enemy mortar men found their range. Explosions with the orange fire and smoke that came with them kept moving ever closer toward them.

"Shit!" Chris looked over at his radioman, Sergeant Comstock, lying next to him. "Radio!" When Comstock didn't move fast enough, Chris yanked the mic off the radio pack. "Tango Charlie six to overwatch." He repeated the words again.

The radio crackled. No one came back with a return call.

Chris handed the mic to Comstock. "Keep trying." He turned to Jefferson. "Have the men move toward that stand of trees. It might give us some cover."

Jefferson belly crawled away to pass the word to the men.

Suddenly, the area got quiet, with an occasional tree limb falling to the ground.

Chris pointed his M16 where he thought the enemy might be, hoping for a target to appear. "Let's move out while we can. I bet they're moving their emplacements."

The men stood and moved in a low crouch below the level of the grass toward the trees. In what seemed like hours but was only a few minutes, they reached the relative safety inside the stand of trees. Safety in that they had more cover than in the tall grass. The trees did have some extent of ballistic protection.

Within seconds of their arrival, a deluge of rocket, mortar, recoilless rifle, and rocket-propelled grenade fire came down in a never-ending onslaught. At least the trees stopped most of it. The rest sailed through, exploding behind them.

Chris felt the splinters hitting the ground around him. It wouldn't be long until the ongoing artillery mortar fire turned the trees into splintered kindling. He felt like a rat in a trap with no way out.

Comstock crawled up next to him. "Sandys on the way, sir. ETA, two minutes.

"Thanks." He turned to Jefferson on the other side. "When the Sandys hit them, we move forward. Have C Company come in from the other direction and squeeze them between us. I want these mother fuckers."

"Done." Jefferson grabbed the radio mic off Comstock's pack.

Chris put a fresh magazine into his M16, charged the weapon, and waited. Time slowed until the buzz of radial engines overflew the trees. Then came the whoosh of rocket engines. The ground rolled from the impact as the area around them turned orange. The explosive pressure sent the trees whipping back and forth. Smoke from the fires covered the area.

He got on his feet, inched forward, and went out into the daylight. His men joined him. The whole area glowed red, orange, and yellow as the napalm fires burned. C Company came over the ridge, guns blazing.

As Chris ran toward the enemy position, firing his M16, the hot barrel smoking in the humid air, he felt something slam into his left leg and take his feet from under him. His rifle flew from his grasp. He fell forward, sliding in the mud on his stomach.

"Medic," someone yelled next to him.

Chris rolled over and looked at Comstock kneeling next to him, strapping a tourniquet high up on his leg, near his crotch. "Don't move, sir."

"Don't intend to," Chris replied. He felt a sharp prick and started feeling woozy. The blue sky turned gray and went dark.

1000 Hours
May 7, 1970
93rd Evacuation Hospital
Long Binh, South Vietnam

Chris looked up from the year-old copy of *National Geographic* magazine when his door opened. Reading helped pass the time.

Colonel Best came in looking spit and polished in his class A uniform with a folder tucked under his arm.

Chris sat up straighter in his bed and put down the magazine. "Sir." *What's going on?*

The colonel smiled. Not a friendly smile. More of a forced professional one. "Relax. You don't have to sit at attention, Patterson."

"Yes, sir." He was still uncomfortable in the presence of the colonel wearing an open-backed, drafty white hospital gown.

"You did an excellent job in Cambodia."

Chris sure didn't think so. He led his men into a trap. "Yes, sir. It's not as bad as it looks." He massaged his left leg propped up on several pillows. It itched under the mound of bandages. The damn morphine made sure he didn't feel any pain. *At least I don't have a Foley anymore. But I wish they'd take out the damn IV.*

"Typical for an Airborne guy. I talked to your doctor. That round did a lot of damage to your thigh. You'll be in the hospital on crutches and healing for two weeks and on injury leave for at least two more."

"Yes, sir. The doc told me already. What happened after I passed out?" He needed to call Kara before she found out some other way. She'd panic at the formal language of the form letter telegram. "We regret to inform you…"

Colonel Best sat in the chair next to the bed. "Captain Jefferson took over. The Sandys did their job, and your men cleaned it up."

Chris swallowed, not wanting to know this but needing to. "How many of my men died?" He hated writing those letters.

"Four with ten wounded. Your men handled themselves well, all things considered. Want to know what you stumbled on?"

"Yes, sir." *Sounds big.*

"A weapons cache manned by a platoon of NVA regulars. Jefferson reported twenty-seven KIA, ten captured, two crew-served weapons, fifty small arms, two recoilless rifles, ten thousand rounds of ammunition, ten mortars, and five hundred pounds of food destroyed."

"That's good, sir." *But was it worth four good men?*

"I'll add it to your growing list. And I put you in for a Purple Heart."

"Yes, sir. Thank you, sir." He didn't want a medal, only out of the hospital and back to his unit.

"Until you're cleared for duty, relax and enjoy the downtime. Once you return, I'll work your butt off…Lieutenant Colonel Patterson."

"Yes, sir…Huh?" *Did he just say, Lieutenant Colonel?*

"You heard me, Patterson. Congratulations on the promotion. You earned it." The colonel handed Chris the folder under his arm. "No more of this." He pointed at the bed.

"No, sir. I intend to avoid hospital stays at all costs." Chris nodded at the door. "The nurses watch everything." He hated peeing into a bedpan in front of a girl. He didn't even do that with his wife. It was embarrassing for them to see his penis, balls, and bare butt hanging out of a hospital gown.

Colonel Best laughed a genuine laugh. "I know. Mine was a bullet in the ass in Korea when an enlisted man in my platoon dropped his rifle. I had to lay on my stomach at the MASH. I cringed when the nurses removed the bandages on my bare ass to clean the wounds. They saw everything."

Now it was Chris' turn to laugh. "Yes, sir." *Guess we all have our bad days.*

0500 Hours
August 17, 1970
1st Cavalry Division Officers Quarters
Phước Vĩnh, South Vietnam

As Chris smoothed the standard green wool Army blanket on his military tight bunk, ready for his morning run, he heard a knock on his door. It didn't sound like Jefferson's usual knock that rattled the doorframe, much too light. "Enter," he called out.

The door drifted open. Standing in the doorway was Staff Sergeant Dworaczyk, assigned to monitor all overnight communications coming from the field. "Sir. I didn't want to disturb you." He held out a piece of paper. "But I bring a message."

"About what?" Chris took the paper.

"Just read it, sir. You left word in the commo room to watch for any information on...Lieutenant Colonel MacKenzie of the 5th Special Forces."

"Jackson?" Chris waved at the door. "Dismissed."

Dworaczyk closed the door.

Chris sat on his bed, his run forgotten. He slowly unfolded the paper, not sure if he really wanted to know if Dworaczyk's reaction was an indication of what's inside.

36

To all US military installations in the Vietnam area of operations:

Subject: Lt. Colonel MacKenzie, US Army, 5th Special Forces Group

On 16 August 1970, Lieutenant Colonel Jackson J. MacKenzie, Major Harrison A. Russell, Captain William L. Mason, 1st Lieutenant Tyler M. Carter, Sergeant First Class Dakota C. Blackwater, and Staff Sergeant Michael P. Roberts, all assigned to the 5th Special Forces Group, were discovered by a long-range patrol of the 101st Airborne in the I Corps south of the Ben Hai River/DMZ.

The men are alive but suffering from malnutrition and injuries from extended captivity as POWs of North Vietnam and recently escaped. They were airlifted to the 95th Evacuation Hospital at Da Nang. The medical prognosis for everyone, with the exception of Lieutenant Colonel MacKenzie, is positive. According to the medic who accompanied them to Da Nang, Lt. Colonel MacKenzie's injuries and malnutrition are so severe that he is not expected to survive.

Updates will be forwarded as received.

USMACV - US Military Assistance Command Vietnam

"Fuck! Geez, what happened to them?" Chris blurted out to no one. At least they all were alive. That was a plus. He could only hope and pray God would allow Jackson to stay that way. He'd already lost a daughter. He didn't want to lose his oldest friend as well.

CHAPTER 10

0800 Hours
August 24, 1970
95th Evacuation Hospital
Da Nang, South Vietnam
I Corps

Chris didn't know what to expect when he entered the hospital. Would they even allow him to see Jackson? He wanted to visit sooner, but the word he received from his request to Dr. McKay was an emphatic *no*. Jackson was in critical condition. This time he came without asking first. Rank did have its advantages with young, impressionable, lower-ranking nurses.

He stopped at the central desk and leaned on the counter in front of a nurse with her head down. Her faded and stained OD green cotton jungle fatigues looked tired like her.

"Lieutenant," Chris said softly to get her attention.

The nurse looked up at him and smiled. "What can I do for you, Colonel?"

"I'm here to see Lieutenant Colonel MacKenzie."

"Are you on the visitation list, sir?" She picked up a clipboard to look for his name.

"There's a list? I'm probably not on it. I haven't been here in years."

"I'll have to ask Dr. McKay. The colonel only gets approved visitors."

"And who are they?"

She ran her finger down the page. "Major Russell, Captain Mason, Lieutenant Carter, Staff Sergeant Roberts, and Sergeant First Class Blackwater."

Figures. "Only his men, huh? Has something happened?"

"Well…ahhh…"

"Lieutenant, what happened?" Her reluctance had him worried.

"CID," said a male voice behind him.

"Huh?" *What does CID have to do with this?* Chris turned to face the man behind him. A doctor from the faded, stained green fatigues, lab coat, and stethoscope hung around his neck. "Something tells me you're Dr. McKay."

"I am." The doctor jabbed his clipboard at him. "Who are you?"

38

"Lieutenant Colonel Chris Patterson."

"Why do you want to see Colonel MacKenzie?" the doctor asked warily.

Chris held up the gold West Point class ring on his right hand. "I went to the academy with him. He was my roommate and my oldest friend. You can have Harry Russell confirm it. I want to check on him."

The doctor tapped his lips. "Okay. For now. Please don't ask what happened to Colonel MacKenzie. CID tried to force it out of him. It upset him so much the stress sent his medical condition into a tailspin. He'll talk when he's ready, and right now, he's not ready."

"Understood." *Why couldn't those fucking bastards wait a few days? Give the man a chance to recover.*

Chris followed the doctor to a room set off from the main recovery ward. "Why's he separated from the others?"

"Privacy. When expectants are brought in, this is where we sometimes bring them to die in private. We believed Colonel MacKenzie wouldn't make it through the night. I had him put in this room and made comfortable. He's got a fighting spirit that won't quit and surprised the hell out of us."

"What were his injuries? All I could get from the report was he and the others escaped from a POW camp. His injuries weren't listed."

"Extreme malnutrition, so he's extremely underweight. When they were brought in, he was right on that fine line of possibly being too far gone to survive. We originally gave him a twenty percent of survival."

"Not good. I take it that's changed."

"It has. By small increments. Given his recovery at this point and his strength of will, I'd say he'll be over the hump in a few days, but he's still on the critical list."

"What else?"

"His intestines were full of parasites, which exacerbated the malnutrition."

That gave Chris the willies. His imagination kicked in, and he could feel things squirming inside his gut. "I take it there's more."

"Much more. We shaved his head to get rid of the lice."

Now Chris' head itched.

"At some point." The doctor paused and swallowed. "They whipped the living shit out of him. His back is a crisscrossed mess of scars."

"Oh my God!" Chris couldn't imagine the kind of pain that entailed.

The doctor continued. "A broken left collarbone. Badly infected cuts all over his body. A half dozen broken ribs, a fungal infection all over his feet, a minor case of malaria and dysentery, and…at some point they broke his left arm. It wasn't set correctly and healed funky."

"That's not exactly a medical term, Doctor. What do you mean by funky?"

"The bones in his forearm are twisted like an old oak tree. I didn't want to attempt such an invasive surgery with him dealing with so many health problems. I'd have to re-break the arm to fix it properly. Maybe in the future when he's stronger. But not now. If it doesn't limit his range of motion, I wouldn't advise having the surgery unless there are future complications."

"Geez, how'd he survive all that?"

"You were his roommate. Surely this isn't the first time you've seen someone go beyond what you think the human body can take."

"Yeah, but that was training in a controlled environment, not this much life and death crap."

"True. Remember my warning."

Chris smiled. "I'm not going to upset him, Doc. Promise. I'm glad he's alive."

"Good. Stay as long as you like. He'll probably enjoy another visitor. I'll have the nurse tell his men to stay away until you leave. They have a rotation going to sit with him during visiting hours.

"He has good friends, Doc. Thanks." Chris opened the door slowly, not wanting to wake Jackson if he was sleeping. What he saw caught him by surprise after everything the doctor had just told him.

Jackson was awake and alert, sitting up in bed propped up on pillows and drinking something from a large moisture-covered glass with a straw. His left arm was strapped immobile to his body. He had the nasogastric feeding tube, IV lines, heart monitor leads, a cannula under his nose, and was wearing thick blue flannel pajamas, not a hospital gown. Jackson's gaunt face and rail-thin body made him look like an Auschwitz survivor.

Slowly, Chris approached the bed, wondering about the contents of the glass. Finally, the smell, color, and consistency told him…chocolate milkshake. *I haven't seen ice cream in six months.*

Jackson wiped his mouth with a napkin. "Chris! What brings you up from Phước Vĩnh? Doesn't the 1st Cav keep you busy?"

Chris pulled up a chair and sat down. "Yes, they keep me busy. But I had to check on you."

"How'd you get past Dr. McKay? He's overly protective."

"Told him the truth. You're my oldest friend and academy roommate."

"Well, that always works." Jackson held out his right hand. "Thanks for coming."

Chris gripped Jackson's trembling hand gently and shook it. "You're welcome."

"I see you finally made rank."

Chris brushed the silver oak leaf on his collar. "Sure did. About three months ago." He pulled Kara's picture from his shirt pocket and handed it to Jackson. "Now, it's my turn. I should've told you this the last time I saw you…but I forgot. I wanted you as my best man for introducing us, but we couldn't wait."

"You got married to Kara? Congratulations. Any children yet?"

Chris swallowed and shook his head. "No."

"What did I say wrong?" Jackson asked, handing the picture back.

"You didn't know. Right before I got my orders for 'Nam, Kara gave birth to a little girl. We picked out the name Amanda Elizabeth." He wiped a tear away. "The cord prolapsed around her throat, and she was…stillborn. Kara can't have any more children."

Jackson gripped Chris' arm. "Chris, I'm sorry I mentioned it."

He's half-dead and comforting me. What a good friend. Chris placed his other hand over Jackson's. "It's okay. I've been carrying around the guilt since I arrived in Vietnam. You're the first person I've told about it."

Jackson looked askance at him. "Why am I so special?"

"You're my oldest and best friend. Who else would I tell? Does your wife know you're here?"

Jackson's happy expression darkened. Chris wondered why. Was he going to get booted out by Dr. McKay for breaking his rules?

"Carolyn divorced me. JAG brought me the paperwork a few days ago. She told the judge I abandoned her when I volunteered for another tour and didn't answer her letters." Jackson slammed his hand on the bed. "That's kinda hard to do beaten and trussed up like a Thanksgiving turkey in a tiger cage."

Chris felt bad for mentioning it. "Shit, now I'm sorry."

Jackson nodded then smiled. "It's okay. I'm tired of stewing about it and getting stuck with damn needles every time something upsets me." He leaned forward and lowered his voice. "Keep this between us."

"You got it." Chris gently gripped Jackson's shoulder. "Get well, knucklehead. Kara wants to have you over for dinner when we get home. Let's not disappoint her." He needed to stop by the base MARS station before leaving Da Nang and call Kara to let her know Jackson was alive and safe.

"Now." Jackson's grin was infectious. "Go lock that door and tell me everything I've missed in the last year, including what the great Athos has been doing."

Chris did as asked, chuckling as he returned to his chair. "Haven't heard that in years, Aramis." He thrust his arm out like he was holding a sword. "One for all—"

Jackson copied him, his fake blade crossing Chris'. "And all for one."

They both loved the Alexandre Dumas book *The Three Musketeers* and acted out the scenes at fencing practice. Chris figured they watched the movie a dozen times together during their four years together at West Point. And dueled in their room with their Firstie swords.

CHAPTER 11

0400 Hours
March 1, 1971
Long Khanh Province
III Corps
South Vietnam

The helicopter inserted Chris's twelve-man rifle squad from A Company five klicks south of their objective. Chris led them down a small creek bed to avoid detection to the village of Song Trâu. The moon in the cloudless sky showed the trail so brightly in the darkness they didn't need any flashlights.

Chris chose to command this mission for a reason. He wanted to get out of headquarters. With the brass bogged down with the 1st Cav's March 26 pullout, they might task him with balancing the logistics. Something he didn't want any part of. The task of bringing thousands of men home at the same time was daunting for even an experienced officer.

Intelligence from Colonel Johnson, commanding officer of the 313th Army Security Agency Battalion in Nha Trang, stated there was a large weapons cache like the one in Phước Long Province inside an abandoned Christian orphanage in Song Trâu. Chris asked Johnson multiple times whether his men in the field had confirmation the building was empty. Every time Johnson reaffirmed that all children were relocated to Biên Hòa and only VC were in the building. With that, Chris gave the go-ahead for the mission.

He belly crawled up the creek bank and looked over the top. His men in their muddy OD green cotton jungle fatigues took up positions to his right and left, their M16s aimed downrange except for the man on rear guard watching their backs. Captain Jefferson lay directly next to his right shoulder. Chris placed his binoculars up to his eyes, adjusting the wheels to see the building clearly.

The old yellow church-style stucco two-story building looked abandoned and run down to the point of collapsing. Several of the glass windows were broken or missing altogether. One of the red front double doors hung sideways on the hinges with the other one closed. The defensive emplacements of concertina wire around the compound weren't in any better shape than the building. The intelligence had obviously been correct. The place was deserted.

Chris scanned the area, but the only thing moving were grass, insects, small animals, and frogs. The frogs kept croaking around them almost in time with the crickets in a weird musical. He waved his men to move forward. Before anyone could move, he saw a puff of smoke and heard a small poof. Ten feet away, something exploded. Chunks of dirt and plant matter flew upward then fell from the sky like hail and raindrops. His heart went into overdrive, thumping hard inside his chest. Ambush. Shit!

Machine guns opened up on them from the broken windows, plowing deep furrows on the highest part of the muddy bank. Rattan mats camouflaged with natural grass flipped up, and more enemy combatants fired in their direction with AK-47s and larger automatic weapons. Mortar fire rained down on them and exploded, sending bits of everything into the air. The mud reeked of mildew, rancid water, and the local fertilizer – human shit. Smoke clouded the area, making it hard to see anything or breathe.

With the intense onslaught of fire, Chris and his men scrambled around, taking cover in any depression they could find behind the creek bank, flattening themselves into the mud with their asses exposed. They could only hope Charlie wasn't behind them.

Chris heaved his M16 over the bank and fired at the muzzle flashes in the smoke. The man with the M60 joined in as the other men let loose with their own barrage of automatic gunfire. The thunderous roar was deafening.

Captain Jefferson raised up on one knee and fired a round from his M79 grenade launcher. He bent down to reload. As he brought the weapon back to his shoulder to fire again, his arms flew outward. The M79 dropped into the mud. Jefferson fell onto his back in the mud with a splat.

"Medic," Chris yelled, belly-crawling to Jefferson's location, his M16 out in front of him, using it to drag himself through the thick mud. He ripped open Jefferson's shirt. The man's chest was nothing but shredded meat with his heart and lungs full of large holes, still, quiet, never to work again.

Chris slammed his fist into the mud. He'd seen men die before, but this was personal. "Fucking gooks. Kill them all."

The unit medic, Sgt. Rogers made his way to them and placed a hand on Jefferson's carotid artery. "He's gone, sir." Rogers pulled Jefferson's body up onto the bank.

Chris nodded. "Radio!"

The radioman, Corporal Lang, ran hunched over to his side. "Colonel."

"Get on the horn. Get us some backup and a fucking airstrike, artillery strike, whatever."

"Yes, sir." Lang pulled the receiver from his pack and put it to his ear.

"Where's—" Chris ducked as a round struck the ground a few feet away, sending a geyser of water and mud into the air. "—Swanson with that rocket launcher?"

Swanson ran over, blood dripping from under his helmet, down his cheek, and off his chin. "Major."

"Are you wounded?"

"Just a small nick, sir. I'm ready to rock and roll."

Chris slammed a fresh magazine into his M16. "Destroy that mother fucking building and everything in it."

"You got it." Swanson hefted the M-72 LAW to his shoulder, quickly aimed, and fired. The fiery backblast made Chris' ears pop.

That round hit the side of the building, causing it to collapse.

Swanson grabbed his second M-72, aimed, and fired. Not only did a wall collapse, but an even larger explosion went off, sending flames and black smoke into the air.

When several VC turned to look behind them, Chris threw two grenades into their trench. Body parts and misted blood erupted into the air, silencing that machine gun and its crew forever.

"Colonel, there's a Marine platoon en route to us, and the Sandys are inbound. Pop a red smoke to mark our position," Lang yelled over the mayhem.

Chris pulled a red smoke canister, pulled the pin, and rolled it in front of him. Red smoke drifted across the creek, blowing away from the building in the breeze.

The two dots in the sky became a pair of camouflage-painted, fixed-wing, propeller-driven aircraft, A-1 Skyraiders, the "Sandys."

The men still alive hunkered down behind the creek bank as the Sandys made their runs at a few feet above the treetops, the roar of their piston-driven engines drowning out everything. First the Napalm canisters fell from the Sandys wing mounts, sending flame and black smoke skyward. Anything alive in the kill zone would now be roasted flesh. Chris could feel the heat on his back.

Rockets, with long streaks of fire streaming from their tails, slammed into the structure. The men held their hands over their ears to protect them from the noise and pressure changes.

Then the Sandys whooshed in at tree-top level with their wing-mounted 20mm cannons blazing. The armor-piercing and incendiary shells burst through the building, and the people, leaving them bloody, burned, and tattered versions of Swiss cheese.

Lang pulled on Chris' shirt sleeve with the radio receiver held to his ear. "They're done, sir. Nothing moving."

"Have them make another pass to make sure," Chris yelled. His ears were still ringing.

The men waited while the Sandys made another low-level strafing run with their wing cannons blazing then climbed back to altitude and circled the area.

"All clear, sir," Lang said, hanging the receiver on his radio pack.

Chris inched his helmeted head above the edge of the creek bank. Thick smoke from the burning fires drifted across the area. Where a building once stood, now there was only rubble. While holding his M16 against his shoulder with his right hand, he motioned with his left for his men to move out. His remaining six men lined up behind him, their rifles held at the ready.

Scanning back and forth, he moved slowly forward, step by slow step. He avoided the bomb craters and holes but pointed his rifle into each one, checking for life. If he found any VC alive, he'd quickly ventilate them. They didn't deserve to live. The burned stench got stronger and stronger as Chris and his men closed in on the remains of the building.

At the shot-up foundation, Chris spotted a man-sized hole and looked inside but saw only darkness. He pulled his flashlight off the shoulder strap of his web gear and shined it into the hole. The scene below came into view as he fanned his light across the expanse, small cots lined up end to end. On those cots, not adults but young children. Their long sleeping tunics were black from soot and scorched due to the fires. The frozen looks on their dead, bloody, chewed-up faces...fear.

"Medic," he yelled, falling to his knees and puking. Not from the burned stench of death but seeing the tiny body of his daughter superimposed over the bodies below. He could already tell none were alive. He was responsible for their deaths. Johnson had been wrong. Or he lied.

1000 Hours
March 3, 1971
1st Cavalry Division Headquarters
Phước Vĩnh, South Vietnam

Chris stood at rigid attention in front of Colonel Best's desk as the colonel paced around him. His boot heels clicked against the floor like thunder.

"I've got another My Lai on my hands. What were you fucking thinking, Patterson?" Best thundered, his face beet red. "I trusted you to take care of this. Why did I give my permission for you to take that mission? Why did I recommend you for accelerated promotion? Got anything to say for yourself?" He stopped nose to nose with Chris.

"Sir, I asked Colonel Johnson if the intelligence boys had confirmed there were no children in the building several times. He told me yes and got mad that I kept asking. This is what I wanted to avoid." Sweat dripped down his back and from his forehead into his eyes, causing them to burn and sting. He didn't dare move to wipe it away. The colonel hadn't released him from the position of attention.

"That's not what Johnson told me. He said the current intelligence only suggested the building was empty. Nothing was definitive."

"But sir—"

"Are you going to say he lied? Or made a mistake?" Best snatched a piece of paper from the desktop, waving it violently in the air. "I've got twelve dead kids and two dead nuns on my hands. The press will crucify us in the eyes of the public. They'll chant My Lai all over again at the peace rallies."

Chris winced. The word *us* meant him. "Yes, sir. But like I said before, Colonel Johnson assured me the children were gone."

"Do you have any witnesses to that statement at the briefing?"

"Yes." Chris swallowed. "Captain Jefferson."

Best slammed his hand on the desktop. "Well, we both know I can't fucking ask him."

"No, sir." Chris had a hard time with this. His orders got not only the children killed but Jefferson and six of his men with two wounded. He spent most of yesterday afternoon writing letters to their families. The one Chris wrote to Jefferson's family was the hardest. Jefferson had talked so much about his family back home that Chris felt he actually knew them.

"Do you know what's next?"

"JAG?"

"Yes. Write up your after-action report...Lieutenant Colonel Patterson. Submit it to me for review. I'll forward it to the base JAG officer. Expect an Article 32 hearing soon to determine your fate."

"Yes, sir. What are my duties other than the after-action report, sir?"

"You're relieved of duty until the hearing." The colonel paused. "Go to the 6th Convalescent Center at Cam Ranh Bay for a full physical."

That order had Chris confused. "Why not here, sir?"

"The docs know you here. I don't want anyone to question the validity of the physical if they find something wrong with you that we can use as an excuse."

Excuse? He's trying to find an angle to get out of this. Make me take all the responsibility. I asked about the children. "I can assure you I'm in full control of my faculties, sir."

"We'll let the doctors determine that. I'll have your orders ready when you bring the after-action report. Until then, you're dismissed, Patterson. Understood?"

"Yes...sir." Chris saluted, turned on his heel, and exited the office. He had to get those condolence letters to the families of his men in the outgoing mail. They were more important than the after-action report.

CHAPTER 12

```
1900 Hours
March 10, 1971
Gunslinger's Bar
U.S. Army Depot
Cam Ranh Bay, South Vietnam
```

Chris stepped up to the water-stained mahogany bar, his jungle boots grinding the ever-present granular bits of sand, dirt, and pebbles into the scuffed wooden planks. The shelf behind the bar contained bottles of every make and kind of alcohol.

High up on the wall hung a painting of a curvy, tanned, well-endowed, beautiful young lady with long blond hair, wearing a fringed buckskin bikini, leather gunbelt, and a pair of pearl-handled Colt Single Action Army six-shooters. The mascot of Gunslingers. He wondered how many soldiers sat on this same stool and drooled over that painting.

An American flag tied to the center support fluttered in the slight breeze from the propped open front door. Flags of the U.S. Navy, Army, Air Force, and Marine Corps decorated the other walls. Even inside a building with open doors and windows, the humidity was oppressive, like breathing underwater.

The bartender placed a small paper napkin in front of Chris. "What are you drinking, Colonel?"

Chris fingered the silver oak leaf on his collar. He might not be for long once JAG finished its investigation. His next stop might be Leavenworth. The doctor in charge of his physical said he was in perfect health. That took Colonel Best's excuse off the table. "Ahhh…scotch on the rocks."

"Great choice, Colonel." The bartender set an ice-and-scotch-filled glass on the paper napkin.

Chris sipped the amber liquid. It was cheap scotch, but right now all he cared about was drinking away his thoughts of dead children. He hadn't been able to sleep since that day.

Halfway through his fourth drink he heard a familiar male voice except he couldn't understand him. He picked up his glass and weaved his way through the tables.

Near the far wall, under the U.S. Army flag, he found who he was looking for, his friend, Lt. Colonel Jackson MacKenzie. He was dressed in new-looking, pressed OD green jungle fatigues that hung on him like potato sacks. His blond hair was in his standard regulation high and tight, but he appeared at least twenty-five pounds underweight. That wasn't good.

Chris wondered why Jackson was back in-country while still recovering from a year-long stint as a POW and almost dying at the hospital. And Jackson had just been awarded the Medal of Honor for saving a Navy SEAL team in 1968. Normal SOP was to send you home permanently, relegated to speeches, parades, recruiting, and celebrity dinner parties on the rubber chicken dinner circuit. But that wasn't how Jackson operated. He was a hard charger. All or nothing.

Chris set his drink on the table next to several open beer cans, a nearly empty bottle of Wild Turkey, a glass of amber liquid, and a Green Beret with a silver oak leaf on the black, yellow, and red 5th Special Forces flash. "Hey, buddy. Didn't expect to see you here. What are you doing back in 'Nam?"

Jackson glared at him. His eyes were swollen, bloodshot, and glazed over. "Why do you care...baby-killer. I heard what you did," he slurred, taking a sloppy slurp from his half-empty glass.

"What did you hear?" That pissed Chris off. All information on what happened was supposed to be classified until after the hearing. Army scuttlebutt traveled faster than the speed of light.

Jackson let out a loud burp. "That you blew up that orphanage on purpose."

Chris clenched his fists. "No, that's not what happened at all. My men were—"

"You're a fucking baby killer."

"Listen, JJ. I didn't have a choice. We were under heavy fire."

"You sure?" Jackson slammed his fist so hard on the table, liquid splashed out of Chris' glass. "It's not the first time you've killed innocents for a victory. You got a pass when you destroyed that village in the highlands. The brass covered your ass."

"Listen, that was a firefight I didn't start. The VC ambushed us."

"And you firebombed and cooked them whole, even the women and children, dickhead. Did it taste good?" Jackson sneered at him. "You're not the same man I knew at West Point. You've changed...for the worst. You're a cold, blood-thirsty, trigger-happy asshole."

"I've changed?" Chris pointed at Jackson. "What about you? I've never seen you like this before."

Jackson stood so fast his chair went flying backward. He threw a wild right hand at Chris' jaw.

Chris sidestepped the punch easily. With Jackson drunk off his ass, it wasn't even close. He grabbed Jackson from behind in a clinch. "Calm down."

"Fuck off." Jackson raised his elbows and broke the hold, spinning around to face Chris with his fists up.

He threw a right toward Chris' jaw. In defense, Chris raised his left arm to block. The throw turned out to be a fake as Jackson threw a flying sidekick into Chris' midsection, knocking him backward a few steps.

Chris fell to his knees with the wind knocked out of him. Jackson advanced, ready to plant an elbow into Chris' neck. Quickly, Chris jumped to his feet with his hands up, but Jackson grabbed him behind the neck, pulling down and planting a knee into his groin.

Chris howled in pain, his knees buckling as he cupped his crotch. His balls were on fire. Someone grabbed him from behind and pulled him from Jackson's hold. At the same time, two other men grabbed Jackson's arms, hauling him backward away from Chris. Jackson fought the men holding him, trying to get at Chris, screaming curses at the top of his voice.

Chris glanced at the man holding him. A man from the 82nd Airborne, Captain Gage. "I'm okay, Skippy. Let me go."

Gage released his hold and pointed at Jackson, who was no longer being held, standing a few feet away, bent over with his hands on his knees, breathing hard. "What's wrong with him?"

"Fucking drunk and stupid." Chris spotted a jagged, broken glass beer bottle on the floor. He grabbed the bottle by the intact neck and launched it in Jackson's direction. It flew in an arc and struck Jackson's left forearm, slicing it open from the elbow to the wrist. He couldn't believe the bottle hit his target and jumped in victory. "Got ya!"

Jackson dropped to his knees, gripping the forearm tightly, trying to stop the free-flowing blood from covering the floor under him. "Thanks a lot, you mother fucking asshole," he raged.

"Hey, when you start a fight, damn well be sure and finish it." Chris stomped out of the building. He couldn't believe what happened. Now he'd lost another friend. But instead of death, like Jefferson, it was to anger and alcohol. For what he didn't know. It couldn't be only the orphanage.

CHAPTER 13

March 20, 1971
1st Cavalry Division Headquarters
Conference Room
Phước Vĩnh, South Vietnam
III Corps

Chris entered the conference room in his green class A uniform, stopped a few feet inside, and looked around, wiping his sweaty hands on his pants. His heart beat like a trip hammer in his chest. This hearing would determine his future in the Army. His assigned JAG lawyer, Major Max Robinson, also in his class A uniform, came in behind him with his briefcase.

Several small tables had replaced the long table. The tables were arranged in a makeshift courtroom setting. One table in front with a chair behind it for the judge. To the left of that table was one witness chair.

About six feet in front and to his left was another table with two chairs and a matching set on the right. Since the convening authority, Colonel Best, slapped a classified designation on the proceedings, the only people seated in the gallery were Colonel Best and a few other staff officers.

Chris and his lawyer sat at the table on his left. As Chris set his cover on the table, the lawyer opened his briefcase and pulled out a few file folders.

Trial counsel, Major Roland Harkness, prepared to present his case at the table opposite them. His assistant, a young Second Lieutenant, arranged folders on the table.

"Please rise," the bailiff, a sergeant, yelled from his post next to the makeshift judge's bench.

The few Army personnel in the room stood as the Hearing Officer, Colonel Hansen, entered and sat behind the front table.

"You may be seated." Colonel Hansen gave a slight nod to Major Harkness. "Is the government ready to proceed?"

"Yes, your honor," Harkness replied.

"Is the defense ready?"

Major Robinson looked at Chris, who nodded, then back at the—for lack of a better word— judge. He was going to judge Chris' guilt or innocence.

"Yes, sir," Robinson said.

"Good," the judge continued. "As you know, this is an investigational hearing to see if there is enough evidence to confer charges of manslaughter and conduct unbecoming an officer on Lieutenant Colonel Patterson. Due to the abbreviated schedule of the 1st Cavalry Division pulling out of Vietnam, please make your statements brief. Major Harkness, you have the floor."

Chris shook his head. *My butt is on the line, and he wants to hurry things along. That's just great.*

Harkness stood. He picked up four folders from the table and presented them to Hansen. "These are Lieutenant Colonel Patterson's own words in his after-action report. The other three are the autopsy report with pictures of one of the children, a young girl, age four, who died of shrapnel wounds, burns, and smoke inhalation like the other children and nuns, scene photographs taken by CID, and the casualty report. I want them entered as prosecution exhibits one, two, three, and four. I think they'll show Colonel Patterson's wanton recklessness."

And he's showing pictures of dead bodies to press home the point I'm guilty. Chris hung his head. *Geez, I'm sunk.*

"So noted. Since Colonel Best provided me with these documents already, I won't waste our time going through them." Hansen set the folders aside. "Anything else?"

Shit! "Can they do that?" Chris whispered to his lawyer.

"Yes, unfortunately. Depending on what happens, I have the option of filing a charge of undue command influence," Major Robinson whispered back.

"No, sir," Harkness replied. "It is the opinion of the government those documents provide enough probable cause to send this case to court-martial with fourteen counts of manslaughter, Article 119, and one count of conduct unbecoming an officer, Article 133."

Hansen turned toward the defense table. "Major Robinson, the floor is now yours."

"Thank you, sir." Robinson stood. "Even though you've received the after-action report from my opponent and the convening authority, it will show that Lieutenant Colonel Patterson's decisions were completely proper and necessary for the information he had at the time to save his men. He asked about the possibility of children several times and was assured by Colonel Johnson each time none were at the location. You cannot hold him accountable for the enemy's actions in putting a weapons cache inside an occupied orphanage, nor can you prosecute him for information not at his disposal. The only people at fault here is the North Vietnamese government for placing those children and nuns in harm's way, using them as de facto human shields."

"Do you have anything to add to the evidence list?"

"Yes." Robinson picked up a folder. "Colonel Johnson's clerk, having been in the office during the briefing, wrote out a deposition for me before being sent stateside earlier this week. I find it strange he went home with four months left on his tour…unless it was to keep me from finding out."

Harkness stood quickly from his chair. "Are you accusing Colonel Johnson of trying to hide something?"

Robinson smiled. "I didn't say that, did I? But if the shoe fits."

Hansen banged his gavel on the table. "Enough! I'll look over it, and if I have questions, I'll contact him directly. Is that all?"

"No," Robinson said. "Colonel Patterson wants to take the stand."

"Is he sure? That puts him under the threat of cross-examination."

Chris stood from his chair. "Yes, I'm sure, your honor. If Major Harkness wants to hear what happened again and again, I'll be happy to tell him. He's read the after-action report, so he knows all about the battle." He turned to Harkness. "Right?"

"Then take the stand, Colonel Patterson," Hansen said.

Chris sat in the chair to Hansen's right. After being sworn in by the bailiff, he recalled for the court Colonel Johnson's briefing and the events of the battle, why he used the M-72s and called in the Sandys. Everything he said was written in the after-action report. Nothing more. He had to stay distant or break down on the stand.

Harkness had a wolf-like smile as he approached the witness stand. "Have you ever called the Vietnamese people, 'gooks'?"

"Of course. Just like everyone else here. I did in Korea too." Chris waited a few seconds. "I bet you've even called them gooks."

"I'm not the one in trouble. Do you hate the Vietnamese people?"

"That's hard to answer since you can't tell the VC from friendlies. In general, the people…ahh…no. The Cong and NVA, yes."

"You just said you can't tell them apart. Do you think all of them are VC? Is that why you fired rockets into an orphanage? And called in the airstrike? To make sure those four and five-year-old children couldn't attack you later? Shoot you? Blow you up?"

"No! I didn't know they were even there. I did all those things to save my men. They were being cut to ribbons. I watched Robinson die. I had a close view of my men dying. I had no other choices," Chris yelled, jabbing his finger at Harkness.

"There are always choices, Colonel Patterson." Harkness turned to Colonel Hansen. "I believe my point has been made." He sat in his chair.

"You're dismissed, Colonel Patterson."

Chris returned to his chair, his heart thundering in his chest, clenching his fists in anger. He let Harkness get to him.

"If there's nothing else, I'll forward my report to the convening authority. Court adjourned."

Robinson placed a hand on Chris' shoulder. "Now we wait."

"Yeah," Chris said. Did he just fuck up? Was he going to prison for the rest of his life?

0900 Hours
March 23, 1971
1st Cavalry Division Headquarters
Phước Vĩnh, South Vietnam
III Corps

Paperwork. Chris hated paperwork. Forms and files covered his desk. That was the only thing the brass allowed him to do while removed from command, awaiting the decision from the judge. With the division leaving Vietnam, his life was a never-ending paperwork nightmare.

His new XO, Captain Mayborne, a young man from Overland Park, Kansas, poked his head around the open door to the office. "Permission to enter, sir?"

"Captain, come on in. I don't stand on formalities if it's important. I like to get my information quickly. What do you need?"

"Colonel Best's clerk sent word. You're wanted in his office ASAP."

Chris checked his appearance in the mirror. He tucked in his pressed OD green jungle fatigue shirt, ran a quick brush through his crew-cut hair and a cloth over his jump boots. They shined like glass since he polished them last night. What else did he have to do in his quarters other than read, listen to music, clean his weapons, and polish his boots?

He felt like a damn plebe, but punishment this time was more than an area tour working off your demerits. Instead of an hour of full dress marching in the cadet area with a rifle on his shoulder, he could be going to prison, probably at hard labor.

Quickly, he made his way to Colonel Best's office, checked in with the clerk, Sergeant Dixon, in the outer office, and waited to be summoned.

The seconds seemed like hours as sweat from the omnipresent humidity ran down his face and neck. If it didn't happen soon, he'd look like a sopping wet sponge by the time he saw the colonel. If the colonel sent word, why did he have to wait?

Ten minutes later, Sergeant Dixon picked up the phone when it rang, listened for a moment, and put the receiver back on the cradle. He got up, went to the inner door, and opened it. "He's ready for you, sir."

Chris marched into the office and came to attention in front of the desk. "Lieutenant Colonel Patterson reporting as ordered, sir."

Sitting behind the desk, Colonel Best nodded. "At ease. Take a seat."

"Yes, sir." Chris sat in the closest chair. He couldn't tell his fate since the colonel had no emotion on his face.

Best picked up a folder. "I received a report from the hearing officer."

"Yes, sir." His heart wanted to explode from his chest. Was he going to be court-martialed and possibly go to prison, be exonerated, or something in-between?

"He read through all the reports." Best paused for a few seconds. "And listened to you. The compassion and conviction in your voice and mannerisms above everything else convinced him you didn't know about the children."

"What's that mean, sir?" Chris asked.

"It means you've been cleared."

The churning knot in his stomach disappeared, replaced by a returning feeling of confidence. He had expected the worse. Quickly, he tamped down on his desire to celebrate. That wouldn't go over well. He'd grab a drink or two at the O club tonight. He had to appear in complete control in front of the general. "What about Colonel Johnson's clerk?"

"Colonel Hansen spoke with him after he'd already made his decision. The clerk's statement backing up your claim of asking about the children several times only sealed that decision for him and the Army in a big red bow."

Chris let out a breath he didn't know he was holding. "What now, sir?"

"That's up to you. We're leaving some units in-country for the continued strong US presence. Your unit, along with the 2nd Battalion, 5th Regiment, 2nd Battalion, 8th Regiment,1st Battalion, 12th Regiment, F Troop, 9th Cavalry and Delta Company, 229th Assault Helicopter Battalion, will make up the 3rd Brigade. Headquarters will move to Biên Hòa after we head stateside to Fort Hood with Phước Vĩnh being a secondary base of operations."

"I want to stay, sir."

"Excellent. You'll remain CO of 1st Battalion and serve as adjunct brigade executive officer for the move until relieved."

"Copy that, sir."

Best leaned back in his chair. "Patterson, I'm sorry I didn't believe you. I took Colonel Johnson at his word, and that was my mistake. He got some bad intel, passed it on, then tried to protect his ass, but JAG doesn't want to pursue it."

"No worries, sir. It's over."

"Good man. Then you're dismissed, Patterson. You've got a lot of work to do moving the 3rd Brigade."

Chris stood, saluted, and headed to his office. He was glad they were moving to Biên Hòa after learning Phước Vĩnh had become the base of operations for Jackson's unit under Colonel Johnson. The last thing he wanted was another run-in with Jackson.

While it might serve to fix their friendship if they actually talked, it might also end in another fight if they didn't. He put a deep slice in Jackson's arm on purpose, and Jackson might hold a nasty grudge. Chris didn't need any more legal troubles after skating on the orphanage if Jackson decided to press charges.

This way, they both avoided each other. With time, Chris might change his mind and try to patch up their friendship. Or Jackson might seek him out to do the same.

Right now, Jackson deserved being under that asshole Colonel Johnson. That experience might knock that chip off Jackson's shoulder and his cocky attitude down a peg or two.

CHAPTER 14

0500 Hours
June 10, 1971
3rd Brigade Headquarters
"GARRYOWEN TASK FORCE"
Biên Hòa, South Vietnam
III Corps

Chris went for his morning run after reveille, hearing the 7th Cavalry Regiment's official song, the Irish tune, *Garryowen*, blasted over the loudspeakers as he traversed their new base at Biên Hòa. He was antsy as he remained the acting XO of the brigade. As a fully activated unit, they'd assumed operational control of the 1st Cavalry Division's operational area. It consisted of Saigon and the eleven surrounding provinces.

Their primary mission was to continue the interdiction of enemy infiltration and supply routes into War Zone D, known as "Cav Country." An area around the Dong Nai River comprised of the southern Phước Long Province, northern Long Khánh Province, northwest Bình Dương Province, and the northeast Biên Hòa Province. For the 5,000 men of the brigade, the 35,000 square miles were a massive challenge to patrol.

While Chris relished the new command experience of a large fighting force, something to pad his Army resume, he hated being deskbound. He preferred to be in the field with his men, leading by example from the front. Gaining medals was never his objective. That's why he stayed in top shape. If they gave one hundred percent, he gave the same. He couldn't do that in an office behind sandbags and guards.

After finishing his five-mile run, he returned to his quarters and dressed in his combat gear to go out with today's patrol. Why not? Up to this point, they'd only been involved in minor skirmishes that didn't amount to much. The officer in charge of the squad, 2nd Lieutenant Cooper, would be shocked when he showed up at the airfield. The kid probably never had a senior officer go on patrol with him.

0900 Hours
Long Khánh Province
South Vietnam
III Corps

The squad spread out in the field tromping down the nearly waist-high elephant grass. The blades, often razor-sharp, cut through many a uniform into a soldier's flesh. Chris knew this from experience, having cut various parts of his anatomy and replacing uniforms more than once. The stuff stung like alcohol being poured on the open wound.

He scanned the dense foliage and the tree line beyond. Nothing seemed to be moving but the grass. Thank goodness.

The men humped through the quilt-like patterns of the water-filled rice paddies. Probably filled with the local's favorite fertilizer, human waste. Yuk. He'd have to take a long hot shower with lots of soap when they got back to the base.

They had to remain ever vigilant for booby traps along the paths. Most of the time, it was safer to go through the paddies instead of around them. No trees for Charlie to use for the bamboo whip, mace, or tiger traps. Explosives and water didn't play well together. So that made the cartilage trap moot. Wet gunpowder wouldn't light.

The men stayed vigilant as they waded through the knee-deep water hiding the ankle-deep mud, making it hard to gain traction. At the edge of the field came a puff of smoke with an audible poof. A few feet to Chris's left was a splash, then a fiery explosion of orange flames and shrapnel. A geyser of mud, water, and chunks of plant matter flew up then came down, drenching him in a muddy sludge. He ran toward the nearest point of high ground and hit the deck with the other men. So much for easy. His elbows landed hard, driving their bony points into the mud as his heart raced into overdrive. Ambush. Shit!

Chris pointed his M16 at the location of the incoming fire, laying down a wall of lead with his men to make Charlie duck. If possible.

Mortar fire hit the ground around them, making it hard to think as his ears rang. Chris looked around for the radioman. They needed immediate extraction. "Radio, radio," he called several times without any response. They were dead meat if something happened to the radio.

Lieutenant Cooper crawled up to him, his face coated with muck. "Got any suggestions, sir?"

"Yeah, let's get the hell out of here. Where's the radio?"

"On the other side of the line. He probably didn't hear you."

"Yeah. Get us a couple of choppers. Have them set down in the middle of this damn fucking paddy. And get the damn gunships over here to give us some cover. Where's the fucking overwatch?"

"Don't know, sir." Lt. Cooper crawled away behind the men to relay the order.

Chris tossed a smoke grenade out in front of him, hoping the gray smoke would obscure Charlie's view enough until the airborne cavalry arrived. *If we don't get out of this quick, we're goners.*

Time slowed as the firefight raged. Neither side could get the upper hand as rounds crossed in both directions. Empty shell casings and magazines piled at his feet. Incessant explosions kept bathing him and the other men in chunks of plant matter, mud, and fetid water that smelled like shit.

Down the line, someone threw a smoke canister. Red smoke drifted across the rice paddy.

The irregular thumping of multiple rotor blades filled the air. You not only heard but bodily felt them simultaneously.

Chris looked over his shoulder. The small moving dark dots in the blue sky became a green AH-1 Cobra gunship with shark's teeth painted on its nose and a tandem-rotor CH-47 Chinook helicopter.

The Cobra peeled off, circled, then began strafing runs along the enemy position with its two 7.62 mm multi-barrel miniguns blazing, chewing large furrows into the mud.

The Chinook entered into a hover behind them and descended. Chris waved at the men to move toward the Chinook as the Cobra made another run. This time using its 70mm rockets. Streaks of flame flashed across the sky as they left the rails, leaving smoke trails in the sky. Explosions rocked the area as the Chinook landed and lowered its rear boarding ramp.

One by one, the men ran up the ramp. A couple of them helped a soldier hobble toward the aircraft with an arm across his shoulder.

Chris backpedaled to the helicopter, firing his rifle on full automatic until it clicked empty. He threw his last smoke grenade to cover their exit and climbed aboard.

Before the ramp raised into a closed position, he watched the Cobra make another run, launching a round of rockets. The fireballs reached treetop level.

The Chinook lifted off and headed toward Biên Hòa. Time to leave.

Chris moved into the main compartment and counted heads. Fourteen. Everyone accounted for. Okay, so it wasn't easy. But they all would live to fight another day. That's all that mattered. No one left behind.

CHAPTER 15

1400 Hours
January 31, 1972
3rd Brigade Headquarters
Biên Hòa, South Vietnam
III Corps

Today was a proud moment for the 7th Regiment. Standing at rigid attention on the raised platform with Brigadier General Charles Thomas, commander of the 3rd Brigade, made Chris' shoulders ache. At the academy, this uncomfortable position was called "bracing," or "grabbing some wrinkles," chin tucked in and shoulders thrown back as far as the human body would allow or sometimes farther. Not that he cared as sweat dripped into his eyes and down the middle of his back. He'd stand like this all day. For once, he was glad to release command to his replacement, Lt. Colonel Trudeau.

In front of the platform, lined up in formation, the men of the 7th Regiment stood at attention. Each varnished wooden pole capped by a silver spearhead finial gripped by the "honor man" held a red over white swallow-tailed guidon designating each platoon and company fluttered in the late afternoon breeze.

The honor guard carrying the flags, guarded on each side by a man shouldering an M16, stood in the exact center, directly in front of the platform. The gold-fringed American and 7th Regimental flag with its battle and campaign streamers. The breeze wasn't strong enough to make the large flags do much more than ripple but the battle streamers, at almost three inches wide and four feet long, took on a life of their own, wiggling like snakes.

Chris knew each one by heart, having seen this flag on its stand in the lobby almost every day since he arrived in-country. The campaign ones - Indian Wars, Mexican Expedition, World War II/Pacific Theater, Korean War, and Vietnam. Thirty-two in all and more to come with no end in sight for the men of the Garryowen Task Force.

The colors wouldn't be "cased," literally furled and placed inside a canvas bag, until the regiment received orders to move then "uncased" at its new station. Hopefully, at Ft. Hood in the near future. The new home of the 1st Cavalry Division.

And the unit awards – Five Presidential Unit Citations, one Philippine Presidential Unit Citation, two ROK Presidential Unit Citations, one Valorous Unit Award, one Chryssoun Aristion Andrias (Bravery Gold Medal of Greece for Korea), and two Republic of Vietnam Cross of Gallantry with Palm.

However, for this ceremony, the general added several more awards to the streamers for actions between 1969 and 1971.

Pomp and circumstance abounded as the general slowly clipped each new streamer to the flagpole. A Valorous Unit Award embroidered FISH HOOK, a Republic of Vietnam Civil Action Honor Medal, First Class, embroidered VIETNAM 1969-1970. Then came a Republic of Vietnam Cross of Gallantry with Palm, embroidered VIETNAM 1969-1970, and another embroidered VIETNAM 1970-1971.

Chris' shoulders were about to fall off by the last one. This activity gave the men a brief respite in the form of a party with cake, beer, good food, and what everyone looked forward to, sleep. At least until the next mission or sapper attack.

But for him, as he patted his pocket, a party was appropriate. It was over for him. He got his orders. He was going home. Finally.

CHAPTER 16

1900 Hours
February 1, 1972
3rd Brigade Headquarters
Biên Hòa, South Vietnam
III Corps

Chris paused while packing his gear into his duffle bag to reread the report. Well, the propaganda statement from the North Vietnamese government. There was nothing official about it. No one types an official document in red ink on browned, dirty-looking paper.

War Crimes sanctioned by the United States Government

On 28 January 1972, during the early morning hours, men of the United States Army broke into the Vietnam National Museum of Fine Arts inside our capital city of Hanoi. They stole four of our most revered paintings and replaced them with fakes for their own monetary gain.

This unconscionable event proves we are not the aggressors. The United States military and their brainwashed followers are not here as liberators as they claim but common thieves who serve as cannon-fodder for ruthless invaders. What other valuables have been stolen from our peaceful country?

The cowardly puppets involved:
Lt. Colonel Jackson J. MacKenzie
Major Harrison A. Russell
Captain William L. Lewis
1st Lieutenant Tyler M. Carter
Staff Sergeant Michael P. Roberts
Sergeant First Class Dakota C. Blackwater.

These men are all Green Berets, a group of mental degenerates ready to plunder, destroy, and trample on the peace-loving people of the world.

These men are considered war criminals in the eyes of the North Vietnamese government. A bounty of $10,000 cash in U.S. dollars has been placed on each man's head. Make your fortune and become heroes of the Communist Party.

Demand the U.S. Government to stop the war and restore peace in S.V.N. now!
Demand immediate repatriation!
Let the Vietnamese people settle their own affairs themselves!

Truyền đơn này thay giấy thông hành
(This leaflet can be used as a safe-conduct pass.)

Chris couldn't believe Jackson would do this. It wasn't in his nature. He folded the paper, placed it in his pocket, and went back to packing. His "freedom bird," a C-130 filled with soldiers en route to Ft. Hood, departed the Biên Hòa airport tomorrow at 0800 hours. He wanted a tasty meal in town, not mess hall food and to get a good night's sleep.

As he folded his faded uniforms and stuffed them on top and between his boots, he couldn't get the propaganda statement out of his mind. Even though they were drawing down troops like the civilians wanted, it put a really deep black eye on the Army. Jackson didn't want the money. Of that, Chris was certain. Why would he do this?

The drunken fight in Cam Ranh Bay kept popping into his mind. Maybe after the POW camp, Jackson had a mental breakdown and didn't understand right from wrong with his men just following his orders. Who knows? He was tortured badly in that camp. It had to do something to him mentally because it sure messed him up physically.

It didn't help that the base at Phước Vĩnh was hit by a mortar attack, and Colonel Johnson died in the attack. To Chris, Johnson was no great loss. The man was a complete moron, prone to obfuscating the truth. But with the HQ completely destroyed and all the files lost, if Jackson had legitimate orders, they were gone too.

Something else stuck in his craw as he secured the duffle bag. How would the North Vietnamese government know their names and ranks unless someone leaked it to them? The last bit of credible information he received from his contact this morning was their UH-1 helicopter, piloted by Jackson, refueled in Plekiu yesterday then dropped off the radar around fifty miles from Phước Vĩnh. That fact came from the fuelers at the airfield. Jackson and his men were currently listed Missing In Action – Location Unknown – Presumed Lost.

```
1000 Hours
February 4, 1972
Robert Gray Army Airfield
Ft. Hood, TX
```

As he walked down the cargo ramp with his duffle bag strap across his shoulder, Chris felt his heart explode with happiness. He was finally back in the United States after refueling problems, weather delays, and listening to airsick soldiers puke into plastic bags. The interior of the plane smelled like an unkempt dive bar bathroom. He knelt and touched the tarmac to make sure it was real, not a dream.

No bands, kisses, flowers, or parades like he remembered going to with his parents as a child to welcome soldiers home after WWII. Just a day like any other, except now he was home. At least he flew into a military airport. He'd heard horror stories about the men on commercial flights getting spit on and even assaulted in the terminals. What a welcome home from war for their honorable service.

"Chris!" yelled a familiar female voice.

Chris looked around until he spotted Kara running across the taxiway toward him, her long dark hair and red dress flowing behind her. He dropped his duffle bag, waiting, then wrapped his arms around her as she sagged into his chest. Her heart thumped against his. It felt good. Warm and inviting. Love radiated from her entire being.

He kissed her deeply, not wanting to move, and enjoyed the moment as the other soldiers filed past him toward the hanger. "I've got three whole days before I have to report in. Let's go home." And relish in each other's company among other things. Tomorrow, he'd visit Amanda's grave and see the headstone in person.

Chris didn't want to tell her about Jackson on the baking hot black asphalt. It would upset her. He didn't want to embarrass her in public. Bad news was something done in the privacy of their quarters and only at the right time. Too many unwanted eyes were watching right now, and too many unwanted ears on the base who may not understand.

They went to the parking lot together. She drove their car, a 1965 blue Oldsmobile Cutlass, to their house in the officer section of base housing. He wanted to enjoy being home again from the passenger seat. And he was about to fall asleep. It had been a long flight.

Chris opened the door, went inside, and dropped his duffle bag in the hall. He walked around, getting used to his house again. The living room with the console TV and stereo as the centerpiece, the mustard yellow tufted back sofa, and two pea-green overstuffed chairs. He hated the colors, but Kara loved them. That's all that mattered.

He moved onto the kitchen. Nothing had changed. Running his finger along the wooden table with four chairs that belonged to his parents, he remembered them smiling at him as he ate their last breakfast together before he shipped out to Army basic training. They died in a tornado outbreak while he was deployed in Korea. Again, the refrigerator was that same awful yellow, but it came with the house as military issue. Nothing he could do about it.

Their bedroom, their private place. The full-sized bed was covered with the colorful quilt his grandmother made for him. The matching pillow shams were propped against the plain wood headboard. Their dresser was bought from the Sears Roebuck catalog on sale. On the end table was their framed wedding picture. He sat on the bed, realizing how much he missed home.

Kara dragged in his duffle bag, leaned it against the wall, and sat next to him. "I got the feeling you wanted to tell me something at the airport."

She read him like a book. "Yeah, I need to tell you about Jackson."

0200 Hours
February 5, 1972
Patterson Residence
Married Officers Housing
Ft. Hood, TX

Scanning back and forth, he moved slowly forward, step by slow step. He avoided the bomb craters and holes but pointed his rifle into each one, checking for life. If he found any VC alive, he'd quickly ventilate them. They didn't deserve to live. The burned stench got stronger and stronger as Chris and his men closed in on the remains of the old yellow church-style stucco two-story building.

Chris spotted a man-sized hole in the shot-up foundation and looked inside but saw only darkness. He pulled his flashlight off the shoulder strap of his web gear and shined the light into the hole. The scene below came into full view as he fanned his light across the expanse, small cots lined up end to end. On those cots, not adults but young children. Their long sleeping tunics were black from the fires. The frozen looks on their dead, bloody, chewed-up faces...fear.

Little pudgy burned oriental baby faces. Boys and girls. Their eyes wide open and staring. Mouths screaming in pain. Screaming in a language he didn't understand. Floating over him. Floating toward him. Grabbing at him. He couldn't get away from the cold, clammy touch of their hands.

"Ahhhhh..." Chris opened his eyes, nauseous, sucking in rapid breaths, his heart thundering, and sweat pouring off his body. He sat up, leaned over the edge of the bed, and threw up.

Kara gripped his bare shoulder. "Chris, you're screaming. What's wrong?"

"Nothing," he said more harshly than he intended. He couldn't keep the anger out of his voice.

"Don't lie to me, honey. What did you see?"

He couldn't tell her about the children. He couldn't tell anyone about the children. Not yet. Maybe not ever.

"Honey, please."

"I can't." Chris got up, grabbed his green robe on the bedstead since he was naked, threw it on, and left the bedroom, careful not to step in the vomit on the floor. He had to make the faces he kept still seeing floating translucently around him go away. With those ghosts following him, he headed for the wet bar in the living room.

Grabbing a bottle of scotch and a glass from the cabinet, he sat in an overstuffed chair next to the window, switched on the lamp, and poured himself a stiff drink. He gulped it down and poured another.

Kara knelt beside the chair in her pink fuzzy bathrobe and grabbed his free hand. "Chris, honey, please talk to me. Don't shut me out."

Chris shook his head. She wouldn't understand. "Just give me some time. I need some time to think to get everything clear in my head. Reason everything out."

"Is it Vietnam? You know drinking is not the answer."

"It is for me." He gripped her hand. "Don't tell anyone. If the Army finds out, I'm toast and up for a psych eval. They could retire me. I don't want to go out that way."

"Are you sure that's not a bad thing?"

Chris shot her a hard look. "Kara!"

"Okay, I won't...for now but that all depends."

"On what?" Chris asked.

"You."

"Thanks." Chris caressed her cheek and took another drink. "I just need some time."

CHAPTER 17

0800 Hours
February 8, 1972
1st Cavalry Division Headquarters
Ft. Hood, TX

Chris set his dress cover next to him on the bench outside the office of the commanding officer of the 1st Cavalry Division, Brigadier General Julius Crass. While Vietnam's humidity was horrible, Texas' dry heat wasn't much better. His green class A dress uniform acted like one of those newfangled weight loss sauna suits as sweat ran down his back. His tie felt like a garrote, tight around his throat.

Quickly, he blew into his free hand and sniffed to make sure no alcohol remained on his breath after having a drink before he left the house to calm his nerves. He placed his service record book in his lap. Waiting to be summoned was the hardest part. You never knew what you were getting into with a new commanding officer, even as a combat-experienced officer. They all had subjective opinions on what comprised the perfect soldier or officer. And no one was perfect.

The minutes ticked by his report time, five, ten. At fifteen minutes, the door opened, and a gruff-looking sergeant major stood there.

"Sorry for the delay, Colonel. The general had to take an important phone call. He's ready for you now."

"Understood, Sergeant." And he did. Many times he had to delay this kind of activity to field a time-critical phone call. Chris stood, handed his SRB to the sergeant, tucked his cover under his arm, and followed the soldier inside.

The sergeant disappeared into the inner office.

Chris waited next to the sergeant's desk. Generals loved all this ceremonial pomposity. He pulled a handkerchief from his pocket and wiped the dust off his Corfam dress shoes to make them shiny again.

A minute or so later, the sergeant exited the inner office and held the door open. "Go in, sir."

Chris straightened his jacket, marched into the office, and came to attention in front of the desk. "Lieutenant Colonel Patterson reporting as ordered, sir."

The general, a balding, stocky older man with a bulbous nose and jowls, opened the file on the desk. His class A uniform strained at the seams. The man needed to do some serious PT before he keeled over from a heart attack or stroke.

"At ease. Take a seat," he ordered.

Chris sat in the only chair in the room, directly in front of the desk. As the general read through what Chris could assume was his SRB, he glanced around the office.

Unlike those in Vietnam, this one was adorned and perfect. Bright white paint on the walls and plush gray carpet under his feet. A large American flag on a highly varnished wooden pole topped by a silver spearhead finial stood in one corner. On a matching pole in the exact opposite corner, the same-sized black flag bore the yellow and black 1st Cavalry patch.

High up on the wall behind the general was an expensive wooden shadow box. Inside was a sword with a brass and nickel-plated scabbard. Chris recognized the sword. The treasured item of a West Point Firstie. A sword with a thirty-inch stainless steel blade etched with U.S.M.A. on one side, brass pommel, and silver grip with a nickel-plated finish. The polished lacquered brass handguard bore a centered West Point Athenian helmet. He had a sword just like it stored in a cardboard box in his garage.

Under the sword were framed photographs of the general with different people, including several presidents and members of Congress, and numerous award certificates. The general, it appeared, loved to show off his accomplishments. It made for great press releases.

The general looked up from the file. "First off, I'm Brigadier General Crass. I like what I see in your service record book, Patterson. Above-average ratings on all your evals. You showed great command and organizational skills in Vietnam. And your bravery is without question." He ran a finger down the page. "Deputy Brigade Commander at West Point. Top ten percent of your class in 1957. Airborne qualified, Special Forces qualified, Combat Infantry Badge, 2nd award. Bronze Star with Valor device in Korea. Silver Star, Soldier's Medal, Purple Heart, Meritorious Service, and two Army Commendation Medals with Valor device during your first tour in Vietnam."

"Yes, sir." He'd heard this exact same speech before from Colonel Best.

"While being part of the Black '57 hasn't affected your career. That orphanage deal kind of knocked you backward for a while."

"Yes, sir." Why did he mention his West Point class' mad dash across The Plain during the graduation parade? He was one of the few who didn't run. The other, though, was a true statement. It did. And probably would keep hanging over his head since the general mentioned it.

"With so many men coming back from Vietnam, I don't have the time for a proper ceremony. You can read the nomination letters yourself." The general pulled a stack of blue presentation cases and black certificate holders from a drawer and set them on the desk. "These are yours. Another Vietnam Service, Bronze Star, Meritorious Service, Purple Heart, the Legion of Merit, Army Achievement Medal, Republic of Vietnam Armed Forces Honor, and Gallantry Cross with Palm Medals. You got the unit awards when General Thomas presented the streamers, correct?"

"Yes, sir." Didn't the general notice he was wearing them above the right pocket of his jacket with his Republic of Korea Presidential Unit Citation? Maybe he thought they were old. But he was looking at his SRB. Who knows how generals think? He wasn't disappointed about the lack of ceremony. Medals not awarded posthumously only made him a lucky soldier.

"Now that we've got the formalities out of the way, I'm assigning you to the 1st Battalion, 8th Cavalry until the 7th returns."

"Yes, sir. Do you know when that might be?" The 8th Regiment was a good unit. He'd make do until his men returned.

"Still undetermined. We were first in. I can see us being last out too."

"Sounds like those blood-sucking politicians." Chris cringed, hoping he didn't misspeak, remembering the same politicians' pictures on the walls.

General Crass gave a strained laugh. "Very true."

Did he just fuck up?

"Do you want to assume your duties now or take some additional leave time since you've been out of the country for two years? You've got sixty days on the books. It's totally up to you."

For Chris, this was an easy decision. He wanted time with his wife and to relax. The nightmares the last few nights at home had him rattled. Kara was all over him about the drinking. He had already been to the liquor store three times to restock the wet bar.

"How about a week, sir?" Chris asked.

"Fine with me." General Crass pointed at his desktop. "I'll take care of the paperwork. If you need another week to get settled in, just call my clerk, and I'll approve it. It must have been tough to leave right after your daughter died. I know what it's like to be away from home for a long time."

"Thank you, sir. If I need to, I'll do that."

"Dismissed."

Chris stood to leave. As he turned, the general cleared his throat.

"Hold on a moment, Colonel," the general asked. "I have something to ask you."

Doing a snap turn, Chris faced the general. "Sir."

Crass handed him a piece of paper. "Have you seen this?"

Confused, Chris took the paper and looked at it. His chest got tight at the words on the page.

To all US military installations in the Vietnam area of operations:

Subject: Lt. Colonel MacKenzie, US Army, 5th Special Forces Group

On 3 February 1971, Lieutenant Colonel Jackson J. MacKenzie, Major Harrison A. Russell, Captain William L. Mason, 1st Lieutenant Tyler M. Carter, Sergeant First Class Dakota C. Blackwater, and Staff Sergeant Michael P. Roberts reported to Lt. Colonel Goodspeed at Phước Vĩnh, South Vietnam.

They were arrested by base security, the paintings recovered, and all five men were processed for transportation to Ft. Bragg via C-130. The ensuing investigation into war crimes perpetrated in North Vietnamese territory and possible court-marshal will be done at Ft Bragg.

We will not be turning these men over to the North Vietnamese government as requested to maintain the peace talks in Paris, France. They are US soldiers and will face military justice in the United States.

Updates will be forwarded as received.

USMACV - US Military Assistance Command Vietnam

At least they're all still alive. That's better than being missing again. And POWs. The NVA would've already executed them. What the fuck is going on? Chris handed the paper back to General Crass. "No, sir." He didn't know what else the general expected him to say.

"Wasn't he your West Point roommate?" the general asked with no emotion on his face.

Does he think I'm involved? Chris nodded. "Yes, all four years, and my oldest friend." *Well, he used to be. The general doesn't need to know about the fight. Unless he already does.*

"Have you spoken to him lately? Any ideas why he would do something like this?"

"No, sir. I haven't seen or spoken to MacKenzie for almost a year. But without any knowledge of what exactly this is, I can't and won't speculate. What's MacKenzie told the investigators?"

"I have no idea. Scuttlebutt is he tried to off himself on the plane ride home. He's been in a coma on a ventilator in the ICU at Bragg for the last three days."

Chris opened his mouth to say something to refute the general's statement then stopped. That probably wouldn't sit well with General Crass to be corrected. Jackson was Catholic. He would never commit suicide. Nothing about this whole situation sounded right, and he'd better stay quiet. His career might depend on it.

"Were you going to say something, Colonel Patterson?" the general asked.

Thinking quickly, Chris nodded. "Only to say, sir, everything is up to CID and JAG to figure out."

"Exactly. You're dismissed."

Chris snapped to attention. "Yes, sir." He left the office, knowing he'd have to use his contacts to find out under the table about whatever mess Jackson had gotten himself into and whether he tried to kill himself. That would say a lot about whether he was guilty or innocent. Was he going to tell Kara? No. Not until he knew the facts of the incident himself. Now he needed a stiff drink. Maybe more. Then he'd have to steel himself for another lecture.

0800 Hours
February 9, 1972
Patterson Residence
Married Officers Housing
Ft. Hood, TX

Ding dong! The loud, clanging bell ripped like a lightning strike through Chris' throbbing head. He opened his eyes, realizing he'd slept in his chair and clothes last night. Kara didn't exit the bedroom. She was mad at him. Again.

Someone rang the doorbell again then knocked hard enough to rattle the door on its hinges. It reminded him of Captain Jefferson's knock. Before going to the door, he finished off the rest of the whiskey in the glass on the end table, burped, and wiped his mouth with his shirt sleeve.

Chris padded to the door in his bare feet and opened it. Standing there was a black Captain, another reminder of Jefferson. He needed a drink. "Yes, Captain," he slurred, not meaning to. He wasn't still drunk, just hungover with a humongous headache. Not a good first impression.

The young man held out a piece of paper. "I'm your new executive officer, sir, Captain Ron Thurman. You left word at the office to have anything that came over the wire about—" he glanced around and lowered his voice. "Lieutenant Colonel MacKenzie delivered to your house while you're on leave." The captain was obviously not pleased with this delivery. His downturned lips and squinted eyes told of his disgust.

"Thanks, Captain." Chris took the note and closed the door. He went to his chair, sat, and put his feet on the hassock to read the memorandum.

> To all US military installations both in the United States and the Vietnam area of operations:
>
> Subject: Lt. Colonel MacKenzie, US Army, 5th Special Forces Group
>
> On 8 February 1972, after a full investigation, Lieutenant Colonel Jackson J. MacKenzie, Captain William L. Mason, 1st Lieutenant Tyler M. Carter, Sergeant First Class Dakota C. Blackwater, and Staff Sergeant Michael P. Roberts were formally charged by JAG under the UCMJ. Article 86 (Absence Without Leave), Article 106 (Impersonating an Officer or Official), Article 129 (Burglary, Unlawful Entry), and

specifically for Lt. Colonel MacKenzie, Article 133 (Conduct Unbecoming an Officer).

Lt. Colonel MacKenzie is currently in the hospital at Ft. Bragg for injuries sustained while inside the territory of North Vietnam. He is under a no-visitor hold. Lt. Colonel MacKenzie is expected to make a full recovery and will be transferred to the stockade once he is determined fit enough for incarceration in maximum security to await court-martial on all charges. Early estimates say two weeks for medical clearance.

Major Harrison A. Russell did not go to the Vietnam National Museum of Fine Arts in Hanoi. He lost his left foot at the ankle in an enemy mortar attack at Phước Vĩnh on 26 January 1972 and is currently stateside admitted to the Los Angeles VA hospital.

The other men are currently incarcerated in maximum security at the Ft. Bragg stockade awaiting court-martial under a no-visitor policy.

Updates will be forwarded as received as this has become a highly sensitive political matter. Most information regarding this case has been deemed – Classified – Need to know – Eyes only.

Pentagon
U.S. Army Chief of Staff – General Windom

Chris dropped the paper into his lap. Jackson was in big trouble with the Army Chief of Staff sending out updates. Why did JAG drop so many bricks on Jackson's head? And what investigation? You can't do that kind of time-intensive investigation in less than two weeks with the only witnesses Jackson and his men. Unless it's a hatchet job. Then time didn't matter.

How could anyone believe North Vietnamese propaganda after the millions of leaflets dropped on them, telling US troops they were fighting for nothing and to desert their posts in protest of the war?

He still didn't believe Jackson did this except under orders. But with his own career teetering on the fine edge of oblivion, he had to make any inquiries into what happened to Jackson on the QT with his contacts in intelligence. Maybe he should contact Harry Russell?

As Jackson's XO, Harry would have the inside scoop about the mission. He was out of the Army's sphere of influence at the VA, which was strange. Harry should still be in an Army hospital, not the VA. But no matter what, Chris didn't want to wind up under JAG or CIDs crosshairs again. This time they might pull the trigger on the charges.

Kara came up next to the chair fully dressed in a green pantsuit with her hair in a ponytail. Her face had light touches of makeup and lipstick. She looked beautiful.

"I'm heading out for an auxiliary meeting. We're hosting a birthday party for a six-year-old boy who lost his father last week." She crossed her arms. "Who was at the door?"

"My new executive officer, Captain Thurman." He debated about showing her the note, but he'd promised to keep her updated about Jackson and held it up. "He brought this."

She read the note. "Geez, Chris. What's going on? Jackson would never commit treason. I went to elementary and junior high school with him. I knew his mom and dad at Camp Pendleton when Dad was stationed there. He loved them and idolized his father. All Jackson ever wanted was to be an officer like his dad. He'd never dishonor his parents or brother like this."

"I know all about his father. He was my West Point roommate. He even wrote a tactics paper about his father's actions at Okinawa based on Marine Corps records and his father's letters and stories. And you're right. He would never commit treason. I can't get publicly involved in this. You know that. All I'm getting is the Army's reports…which I'm sure will stop soon."

"Why?" Kara asked.

"They've classified the entire matter." Chris stood and kissed her cheek. "Go do what you gotta do." He wanted her out of the house so he could pee, get dressed, and run to the liquor store before she returned. He'd drunk everything last night.

CHAPTER 18

Chris heard loud thunks, more like felt them as the crawlspace rattled, and glass breaking somewhere in the house. Last night, yesterday, and the last several days were hazy, like a thick fog between him and the memories. He washed his hands and exited the bathroom. He smelled horrible, like his body had been coated in sweat-soaked three-day-old stale booze. He'd take a shower after he figured out what was going on.

He checked the master bedroom, empty, the bed unmade and rumpled. The living room was also empty. What he did notice, several lampshades were askew, unleveled framed paintings and pictures, and the wet bar cabinet doors were open with dirty glasses on the counter and the shelves empty.

Another loud crash of glass breaking. This time he pinpointed the sound. It came from the kitchen. Did Kara fall? Was she hurt and couldn't call for help?

Chris ran into the kitchen and came to a bare-footed sliding stop on the tile. He stood there and watched Kara pour a bottle of Jack Daniels into the sink then chuck the bottle into the nearby trash can so hard it broke. She picked up another bottle, removed the cap, and tilted it up to pour.

He covered the distance in two steps and caught her wrist, stopping her before any liquid came out of the bottle. "What are you doing? This stuff ain't cheap."

"Saving your life. Let me go." Kara tried to jerk her arm from his grasp.

"Saving my life? I'm fine."

"Have you looked at yourself lately?"

"Why? I'm relaxing."

"Relaxing? Honey, you're hurting me," Kara pleaded.

Chris looked at her wrist with his hand closed tightly around it. Her skin seemed bloodlessly white. He released his grip. His fingers left red marks on her skin. "I'm sorry."

"I want to believe that, but you've drunk yourself into a stupor every day since that nightmare. Do you know how much vomit I've cleaned up for the last week? I've been on my knees more than my feet."

"I thought you liked that."

Kara slapped him hard. "Did you really say that? Not when you're drunk off your ass, buster. Do you realize you're only wearing some really ratty boxers and the blinds are open?"

His cheek stinging with hundreds of fiery needles, he looked down. Not only was he just wearing a pair of frayed white boxer shorts, but his penis and hairy balls were also hanging through the open fly. Feeling the heat rise in his face and ears, he quickly tucked everything back inside. He was not only embarrassed but ashamed about insulting his wife. What was he thinking?

"My father had a favorite saying. Manners maketh man." She picked up a hand mirror off the counter and held it up to him. "You're showing me the exact opposite. Look at yourself. Is that normal?"

Chris leaned forward to see his reflection. His eyes were swollen and bloodshot. He had at least a four-day growth of facial hair. His short sandy brown hair stuck up everywhere. Specks of vomit were stuck to his chest hairs. And the odor that hit his nose could wake the dead. He smelled like one of those decomposing NVA corpses he saw all over Vietnam. No, that didn't look normal. "I'm sorry."

"Stop saying I'm sorry. I know you're not the same man I married after being in that hellhole. I can see it, feel it, and hear the number of curse words that leave your mouth. Smell it. Do something about it. Talk to me."

"Honey, I—"

Kara placed her finger on his lips. "Don't say okay." She pulled out one of the chairs from the table. "Sit."

Chris complied. He didn't want to argue with a splitting headache and a cramping gut that felt like razor blades rolling around inside a washing machine basket.

She pulled a chair around to sit next to him. "I know the drinking seems like a pathway to freedom but it's not. It's a road to self-destruction. Please, talk to me."

He sucked in a deep breath and started shivering. "I feel terrible. What's wrong with me?"

Kara took off her robe and placed it over his bare shoulders. "Withdrawals. Since we have the time…"

If the withdrawals were already this bad, he'd take more leave time. He'd suffer through it at home. It was his fault. He couldn't go to the hospital or see a doctor. The Army couldn't find out about this.

Knowing she wouldn't leave him alone until he told her everything, he grabbed both of her hands for strength. Then everything started spilling out, and he couldn't stop it. He began with the orphanage and ended with his fight with Jackson. If he cried, so be it. He had to get it out any way he could to relieve the pressure or wind up in a drunk, divorced slob in the nuthouse. Hopefully, the nightmares and flashbacks would slow down and stop. He wasn't sure what he was going to do if they didn't.

CHAPTER 19

0900 Hours
March 20, 1972
Department of Human Services
Killeen, TX

"Honey, sit down," Kara called out from her chair against the lobby window.

Chris glanced over his shoulder from reading the minimum wage notice on the bulletin board. This was a typical lobby in a government office – white walls, a check-in desk, and boring. "I don't want to get my uniform wrinkled." He straightened his green class A uniform jacket as proof. It was a partially true statement after spending two hours last night making sure everything looked perfect. He used a ruler to make sure his jump wings, 2nd award Combat Infantry Badge, unit awards, and ribbons were perfectly aligned.

For thirty minutes, he worked on his Corfam black dress shoes until they shined like expensive glass mirrors and wiped every fingerprint off the black brim of his cover. He clipped the Irish pennants off his jacket, taking special care of the eight overseas service bars on his right sleeve, the one item that spoke of his multiple tours of combat duty. Korea and Vietnam. And he ironed his pants until the creases would cut paper.

"Chris, simply sitting in a chair isn't going to destroy your hard work. You look terrific. All spit-polished. You're acting like a recruit on his first day of basic training before meeting the drill sergeant…nervous as hell. Is that the image you want to project for the investigator?"

"No." Chris walked over to the row of plastic, uncomfortable-looking white bowl chairs and sat next to her. Whoever ordered these things did it on purpose, either to make people fidget or because they were cheap. Probably the latter. It was a government entity. But the first option could be a good reason too.

He picked up a magazine from the stack on the next chair, *Time* – May 1, 1972. It has President Nixon's picture with silhouettes of planes and an aircraft carrier on the cover. The caption, in black, on a diagonal red outlined South Vietnam yellow stripe on the right corner, *Nixon at War*. He tossed it back in the pile. The last thing he wanted to read about was Vietnam, having just left that God-forsaken country.

The hands of the clock seemed to spin in slow motion as they waited for their appointment time – 0930. Kara came prepared with a paperback book. A romance from the cover art – a bare-chested well-built muscular man and a scantily clad woman entwined in each other's arms.

Maybe that could be them tonight? Chris had kept his promise. He hadn't touched a drop of alcohol since the day Kara poured it all out. The ensuing rotten hangover headache, jitters, nausea – complete with puke, and anxiety almost sent him back into the bottle for relief. But if he'd done that, she would've left him for sure. He couldn't and wouldn't allow that to happen. She was all he had left.

With her calm assurances everything would be okay, her holding him tight in his arms until the DTs passed, and her love for him, he stuck it out. He even talked about some of what he saw and felt in Vietnam. The battles he participated in. Through that, he felt their love actually deepened. A weight lifted from his heart.

Chris checked the wall clock, 0928 hours. Why couldn't someone come to get them two minutes early? It's not like this place was busy.

At precisely 0930 hours, a middle-aged man dressed in a rumpled black suit exited the one door into the back. The guy seemed a bit of a weasel with greased back hair and a hawkish nose. "Mr. and Mrs. Patterson."

Chris rolled his eyes. They were the only ones in the lobby. "Here," he called out.

"Come with me," the man said with no emotion.

They followed him to an office toward the back of the building and sat in the same chairs as the lobby placed in front of the standard-issue metal desk. White walls with a white tile floor and water-stained textured drop ceiling with flickering tube yellowed fluorescent lights. No adornments on the walls. The cubicle was as sterile as their escort, who sat in a comfortable, padded rolling chair with arms on the other side of the desk and opened a manila folder.

"My name is Wendell Fageto. I'm your case officer. I've looked over your adoption application. I have a few questions," he said, monotone, no hint of personality. Chris could put a finger on his attitude from his mannerisms, clipped and formal. He'd seen it in a few enlisted men in 'Nam attached to other units. Without question, it was hostile.

"Ask away," Chris replied. "We've got nothing to hide."

"Good. I've checked into Mrs. Patterson's background. It's clean, with no dings anywhere. Excellent financials. She's an active member of the Fort Hood Auxiliary and Activity League."

Chris was proud of Kara. She handled everything with skill and dedication during his absence.

"The Army has been very cooperative in my request for records," Fageto continued. "You've got an impressive record...ahhh...Lieutenant Colonel Patterson."

Chris was taken aback by the pause. Did he just read his rank? Had he even looked at their application except for their names until now? Fageto seemed preoccupied with Kara, scanning her up and down, his gaze always landing on her breasts. Under normal circumstances, Chris would tell Fageto to knock it off, but not today in his realm of influence.

"Thanks." That was all Chris could say. But that wasn't a question.

Fageto flipped through several pages. "West Point. Near the top of your class. Numerous awards and commendations for bravery. Service in Korea with the 3rd Infantry Division. Three tours in Vietnam, one with the 82nd Airborne and two with the 1st Cavalry Division."

Still no questions. Just a recitation of his service record. Why? What's his point?

"Now, I have a concern about these records."

"What records?" Chris asked, straightening in his chair. That sounded almost accusatory.

"First, you and your wife lost a daughter before you deployed to Vietnam."

Chris looked over at Kara then back at Fageto. "Yes. We put that on our application. Kara can't have any more children. That's why we applied to adopt a child. We don't care about the sex. Boy or girl, it doesn't matter. We want to give a needy child a good home."

"And that's the reason for this process. Do you think the loss of your child had anything to do with what happened on March 1st, 1971?"

That date was burned into Chris' memory. "Hell, no!"

Kara grabbed his arm. "Chris, you promised."

Chris patted her hand. "No cursing. Yeah, sorry." He looked Fageto straight in the eyes, bristling up at the veiled accusation. "What does that have to do with anything? I was ordered on a mission. We got bad intel. I'm sorry those kids died." *You don't know how much it haunts me.* "But I can't change it. And given the amount of massive firepower we were under, I'd do it again to save my men's lives. The VC put those kids in danger by using them as human shields, not me."

"That may be, Colonel. But it is my decision not to approve your application."

Chris slammed both hands down on the desk. "Why?"

"For the exact reason you're leaning over into my face, trying to intimidate me. You are a loose cannon who makes rash decisions in the heat of the moment."

"Rash decisions. I make logical decisions. You weren't there. What right do you have to judge me without the facts?"

Fageto held up a piece of paper. "These. While the Army cleared you of any wrongdoing for the orphanage fiasco, we don't feel a child would be safe around you." He returned the paper to the file.

"Why?" Chris demanded. Then he saw the outline of a peace symbol on a chain under the man's white button-up shirt. He was a damn war hater, a peacenik. Now he understood his earlier hint of apprehension. The man probably camped out at the airport to spit on soldiers coming home. "Because of the orphanage or that I'm a Vietnam veteran?"

"Both." Fageto smiled. "You could snap at any time. It's been known to happen."

"I'm as sane as you or saner after what I went through. You sat like a fat slob at a desk while I fought for this country. I want to appeal to your supervisor. All the way to the top if I have to."

"You have that right...but it won't make any difference."

Chris held out his hand. "Just give me whatever forms I have to fill out. This isn't the end of our application. You can bet on it."

Fageto handed him a stack of blank forms. "It is for me. I'm going to forward my decision to every DHS office in the United States. You won't get another interview anywhere. I don't think the private ones will take a chance on you either."

"We'll see about that." Chris stood and grabbed Kara's hand. "Let's go home and call the base JAG office. They specialize in assholes who try to screw over soldiers."

CHAPTER 20

0800 Hours
June 29, 1972
1st Cavalry Division Headquarters
8th Regiment Office
Ft. Hood, TX

Every member of the First Team was finally home from Vietnam. Even though Chris was still the commanding officer of the 8th Regiment, he went down to the parade field to watch the uncasing of the 7th Regiment's flag. The same flag he watched General Thomas add all those battle streamers to right before Chris left Vietnam.

He recognized almost every man standing at attention on the parade field in their faded green jungle fatigues. Badges of honor for their service. They stood out from the new men assigned to the division in their unfaded, newer, never seen combat, dark green jungle fatigues.

Chris was proud of his men and would always be a member of the 7th no matter where he went in the future. He was proud to wear the 1st Cavalry patch on his left shoulder, and when the time came to change commands, he'd replace the 3rd Infantry patch on his right shoulder to his new combat patch, the 1st Cavalry Division. The First Team. And as General Cross predicted. They were first in and last out, the first division in Vietnam, and the last to leave. Of course. They were the best.

General Cross added two more Republic of Vietnam Cross of Gallantry with Palm streamers to the 1st Battalion's guidon for a total of five. His troopers did him proud.

After the ceremony, the men scattered, heading toward the refreshments or gathering with their families in the bleachers.

Chris went back to his office. He hadn't heard a thing about Jackson since February 9th. Classified. With the brass out of the building, he had free rein to snoop around in the official communiques in the commo room. Not that he didn't have clearance. He felt like a spy in the movies.

Putting on a poker face, Chris marched into the communications office and stopped at the counter. When the one sergeant on duty didn't look up, Chris cleared his throat. "Ahem."

The sergeant popped up from his chair. "What can I do for you, Colonel?"

"At ease. I need to look through the communications log."

"Yes, sir." The man pulled a hard-sided green notebook from a drawer and placed it on the counter. "Anything else, sir?"

"No, I can find anything I need. Go back to your duties." He didn't need the sergeant looking over his shoulder and telling someone what he pulled from the files.

Starting with February 10th, he ran his finger down the page. On February 22nd, he found one about Jackson being transferred from the hospital to the stockade. From that point on until today, they became sporadic, with a reference on April 1st about Harry Russell being denied access to the stockade.

Not a surprise with Colonel Norville Hammond in charge of the 525th Military Intelligence Group. Chris met him once at a retirement party. The guy was a pompous asshole who didn't belong in Intelligence unless he was looking for it, hoping for a brain transplant. He should be on permanent latrine duty.

The last report listed was on June 1st concerning a Dr. Howard complaining about Jackson's treatment. Those filed messages weren't helpful and brought on more questions. Why was Dr. Howard concerned? Was Jackson sick? What was going on?

Since the brass never stayed long at these functions, Chris handed the notebook back to the duty sergeant and returned to his office. He'd have to follow up with his contacts and hope no one reported him.

1800 Hours
July 4, 1972
Community Center Park
Killeen, TX

Patting his stomach, Chris lay back with his arm behind his head on the red plaid blanket spread out on the lush green grass of the new Community Center Park. The sky above him was clear blue with only an occasional fluffy cloud floating by. Kara's ham sandwiches, homemade coleslaw, and mustard potato salad tasted better than a steak and lobster dinner. Being out of uniform in shorts, a t-shirt, and sneakers felt like being wrapped in soft cotton rather than the itchy, starched stiff boards of his fatigues.

Kara joined him on the blanket, her light blue sundress skirt ruffling in the light summer breeze. He leaned over, kissed her then gripped her hand. This was heaven.

"What are we going to do about the DHS? They won the case and our appeal," Kara asked.

Chris took a deep breath. "I don't know. The JAG lawyer said we don't have any options."

"We could find a surrogate."

"And I have sex with her? No. I can't do that. I'd feel unfaithful to you."

"Even with my permission so we can have a child?"

"My answer is still the same." Chris caressed her hair. "I only want you."

Kara rolled onto her side with her head propped on her hand. "Do you remember my father's favorite saying?"

Chris matched her position as he thought about the question. It seemed familiar but he couldn't come up with the answer. "No."

"I did tell you while you were drunk. Hands and knees."

That he recognized. Well, he remembered the slap. Then it came to him. "Ahhh…Manners maketh man?"

"That's the one. Your faithfulness to me says now you really are the man I married."

"Which means?"

"A good man has a strong sense of what's right and wrong."

"Are you sure of that after what I did in Vietnam? I killed people." He swallowed. "And little kids. Babies. It's why DHS denied our application."

Kara placed her hand on his chest over his heart. "Yes, because under my hand beats who you are. A man with feelings and morals. You killed, yes. But you are not a murderer. As for the kids, that wasn't your fault. Remember that, my love."

As long as he had her support about the orphanage, that was all that mattered. DHS could stick it for all he cared. If having children wasn't part of their destiny, they had each other. That's what mattered.

"What do you want to do until the fireworks?" he asked.

"Relax, enjoy the sun and each other."

Chris wrapped his arms around her waist as Kara flipped around to face the same direction. They cuddled like spoons with his face in her fresh-smelling hair. He closed his eyes, content in this position.

Boom…boom…boom! The ground vibrated violently like a massive earthquake. The air felt electrically charged. Chris could smell smoke, nitroglycerin, gunpowder, gasoline, blood, cooked flesh, and feel burning heat flash over his head.

"Attack! Take cover!" he yelled over the next explosion, trying to climb to his feet to find his M16 or any weapon to protect himself but something kept pulling him back down in rapid jerks.

The black sky overhead lit up with white and red bright flashes. Thousands of multicolored contrails fell toward the ground. They faded out then another explosion and another blinding flash in the sky.

Chris kept trying to stand. Who had him? He had to get to a foxhole before Charlie overran his position. Figuring that had already happened, he lifted his leg to drive his boot heel into the man's head. "Someone help to get this guy off me. Kill this God damn mother fucker," he yelled.

As he lifted his leg, he heard, "Chris, wake up," in a high-pitched female voice that sounded like his wife, but Kara was home, not Vietnam. He stopped mid-way, dropping to his knees, confused. Where was he?

"Chris, wake up," the voice kept repeating.

Blinking, trying to clear the fog away from his eyes, he looked down at his hand, caught in the grip of a smaller hand. A soft-looking female hand with red-painted fingernails. Huh?

"Chris, it's me. Kara," the voice said.

The dense jungle of Vietnam faded into a semi-dark warm night as the sky lit up overhead with a pop. He covered his head with his arms to protect his head from the flying shrapnel.

"Someone shook his shoulders violently. "Chris, look at me," the Kara-sounding voice said.

Chris uncovered his head and looked up at Kara. "Huh?" His heart thundered in his chest and ears. He broke out in a cold sweat.

"It's fireworks, honey. You're home."

"Fireworks, not artillery?"

Kara smiled, smoothing his hair. "Not artillery." She embraced him in a tight hug. "Are you with me now?"

Chris swallowed. "Yeah, think so." He looked around at other couples and families sitting on blankets looking up at the sky, "oohing and awwing" at the bright, sparkling lights.

"I think coming here was a mistake," Kara said.

"Me too. I didn't know it would affect me like this." Chris stood shakily, gathering up their blanket in his arms. "Let's go home. Next year, we skip the fireworks." Vietnam screwed him up good. Would he still be able to function as an Infantry officer if he couldn't take a simple fireworks display and not freak out?

1600 Hours
August 8, 1972
Patterson Residence
Married Officers Housing
Ft. Hood, TX

Chris tossed his keys and cover on the end table next to the couch. "Kara, I'm home."

Kara came out of the kitchen into the living room, wiping her hands on a dishtowel with an apron over her white blouse and gray trousers. "I wasn't expecting you until 1700."

"Took off an hour early with all my paperwork done. How about we go paint the town tonight?"

"I have dinner on the stove, but how about this instead?" She rummaged through her purse on the couch and held up two stiff slips of paper. "I ran into town and got these."

"What are they?"

"Movie tickets for the feature at the Texas Theatre tonight. You know, the cozy one at 320 E. Avenue next to the Ritz."

"Yeah, we went there to see that John Wayne flick, *Hellfighters,* where he plays the guy who puts out oil well fires. We missed most of the movie making out until the lights came up. What movie did you get tickets for?" They could do the same thing in the darkness during the movie.

Kara snickered. "I wanted to make it up to you after July 4th. It's a comedy called *Everything You Always Wanted to Know About Sex But Were Afraid to Ask.*"

"A comedy? You're pulling my leg. There's really a movie with that title?"

"Yes. Seems there's a manual too."

"Okay." Chris gathered her up in a hug. "Let's see the movie and if we like it, buy the book. Not that I need any extra instruction. I've got the mechanics of the subject down pat."

Kara lightly slapped his shoulder. "That's more like my wise-cracking husband. Get out of that uniform and into some civvies. We'll eat here. I want some hot buttered popcorn, chocolate-covered peanuts, and a Coke at the movie."

"So do I." Chris smiled. "You know how to get me in the mood."

Angel Giacomo

2100 Hours
Texas Theatre
320 E. Avenue
Killeen, TX 76541

Holding onto his side with one hand and gripping their still partially-filled large popcorn bucket with the other, Chris exited the theater. He hadn't laughed that hard in years. After hearing the title, even though Kara said it was a comedy, he expected something more serious. It was a pleasant surprise.

The best part was the finale. He loved seeing the sperm bank operator, Tony Randall, release the dressed-as-a-sperm, Woody Allen, who then ran into a four-hundred-foot diaphragm. While Kara laughed through the entire movie, she did get a weird look on her face during the part about *Why some women have trouble reaching orgasm*. Not that she ever did with him at the helm.

Chris stopped when a young man with long, stringy, dirty-looking blond hair, faded jeans, and a tie-dyed shirt stepped into his path.

"I recognize you from the newspapers," the man said in a voice reminiscent of a squeaky mouse. "You're that Patterson dude that killed all those kids and a couple of nuns. What are you doing roaming the earth and enjoying yourself while those kids rot in the ground?"

Kara slipped her arm around his waist. He did the same to fight the urge to slug the kid across the jaw. Thank goodness he held the popcorn bucket in his other hand, or he probably already would have. Infantry soldiers weren't known for long bouts of tolerance.

"I was cleared due to inaccurate intelligence. Listen, son, you don't know what happened. Let it go," Chris said, fighting hard to keep the bitterness out of his voice. He dreamed of those kids almost every night. They wouldn't leave him alone in peace. In his heart, he knew it wasn't his fault, but he still gave the orders that killed them. He didn't need a snot-nosed hippy punk reminding him.

"I'm not your son, baby killer." The man sneered at him. "Did they give a medal or two for killing kids?"

Chris felt his ire rising as a crowd gathered around them. "Of course not. I don't know what you've heard on the news. All I did was try to keep my men alive. We're soldiers doing a hard job. I didn't have a choice that day."

"So says the baby killer. My Lai. My Lai." The man poked Chris in the chest. "Bet you were there."

89

It took all of Chris' willpower to keep from pummeling the guy like a heavy bag. "I wasn't even in-country when that happened. I was at Fort Hood. That was men in the 23rd Infantry Division. No one should ever kill innocent civilians on purpose."

"You did!"

"No. I didn't know about the children until after the battle was over. I was told only the VC occupied the building."

"Yeah, yeah, keep giving me some lame-ass excuse." The man slapped the popcorn bucket out of Chris' hand, scattering the kernels across the red-carpeted floor. "You're a murderer with no conscience. You're deflecting blame onto people who couldn't defend themselves. Does that blood lust give you a hard-on?"

Kara stiffened and took a step forward, clenching her fists. "What did you say? Don't you dare insult my husband."

Chris pulled her back. She clearly wanted a piece of this asshole. "Honey, no. He's not worth it."

"So you're a coward in public, letting your old lady defend you," the man said, waving his arms at the crowd. "See what we get from our tax dollars. Brainwashed cowards who kill peaceful people but don't have the gumption to fight someone who can fight back. Did the Army cut away your manhood? Make you a eunuch robot to do their bidding."

Chris saw red. He pushed Kara behind him and brought up his fists. "Let's find out." He wouldn't swing first, but he'd sure defend himself.

The man bounced around on his feet in front of Chris, bobbing and weaving, faking a few punches to goad him into swinging. Chris stood there with his hands up. While he hadn't boxed since West Point, he could tell a lousy feint when he saw it.

The manager pushed his way through the crowd and stood between them with his hands out. "I've called the police." He turned to the young man. "This is the last time you do this to my military patrons. Get your fucking hippy ass out of here before I have you arrested for trespassing."

The man flipped him the bird, turned, took a step, then turned back and spat at them. The lugie landed on Chris' sleeve.

Before Chris could move, the man ran through the exit doors. With the show gone, the crowd around them dissipated.

The manager pulled a handkerchief from his pocket and wiped at the wet spot. "I'm so sorry. Can I make it up to you?"

Chris knew this happened to soldiers across the country. Some got it even worse, having feces and urine dumped on them. But this was his first experience with it. The kid's words stung his heart. He still dealt with what happened that day and probably would for the rest of his life. All he could do was learn to live with it. He went over and picked up the popcorn bucket. "Can you fill this back up?" They were going to take the leftovers home and eat it while watching the late movie.

The manager seemed surprised at the simple request. "Sure. I'll get you a new bucket and throw in two Cokes and a box of chocolate-covered peanuts."

"You don't have to do that, but thanks." Chris threw the semi-crushed bucket into the trash can.

Kara looped her arm around his waist. "You're a saint. You know that?"

"Not really." Chris smiled. "He wasn't worth being arrested, going through another Article 32 hearing, and possibly going to prison. Once was enough for me."

CHAPTER 21

1900 Hours
December 25, 1972
Patterson Residence
Married Officers Housing
Ft. Hood, TX

Chris sat at the kitchen table. He surveyed the food Kara had prepared for their Christmas dinner. It surpassed his wildest dreams. A small prime rib roast cooked medium-rare. Pink juices coated the platter under the roast. The mashed potatoes were smooth and perfect. She blended the cooked potatoes with fresh butter and heavy cream. A bowl of au jus made from the roast drippings. Rounding out the meal, a salad, cranberry sauce, rolls, and sweet potatoes covered in toasted marshmallows. For dessert, pecan pie from the local bakery.

On the table beside their plates, a wine glass filled with Cabernet Sauvignon. Chris limited himself to one glass. He didn't want a repeat of the past.

The house smelled of cinnamon and vanilla from the lit candles on the counter. Combined with dinner, the scents were delightful. It made this Christmas feel almost heavenly. Of all the days Chris wished for a fireplace, today was one of them. The candles would have to do. They gave the room a flickering ambiance.

The taste of the meal exceeded its appearance. Chris felt twenty pounds heavier as they put everything away and washed the dishes.

They went into the living room and sat in their chairs, holding hands as Christmas music played on the stereo.

Chris admired the tree Kara decorated in the corner. A five-foot blue spruce he bought at the hardware store lot. She covered it with blinking multi-colored electric lights, gold garland, red glass ball ornaments, and silver tinsel. The star on top glowed in tiny white lights.

For several minutes they remained motionless.

"Are you still alive, Chris?" Kara asked.

"Yeah. Just loving being home for the holidays." Chris went to the tree and retrieved a package wrapped in green paper. He handed it to Kara.

"Get yours too."

"Open it."

92

"We do it together," Kara demanded. "We've opened them apart for the last three years."

"Okay." Chris picked up his package, wrapped in Santa Claus paper, from under the tree and sat in his chair. "Go!"

Almost simultaneously, they ripped off the paper.

Kara held up an Australian opal pendant on a gold chain. It sparkled in a colorful subterfuge of three-dimensional fluorescence of different colored images. "It's beautiful. You spent too much."

"No, I didn't. Who else would I spend it on?" Chris placed an Omega stainless steel Seamaster wristwatch beside the opal. "Look who's talking. This thing cost a bundle."

"I wanted you to have something nice besides that crappy beat-up Army issue watch you always wear."

Chris changed watches, placing his Army one in the box. "Here, let me." He held out his hand.

She handed him the necklace and turned.

He placed it around her neck then spun her around. "Merry Christmas. I love you."

"I love you too." She tilted her head, and he kissed her. This was the best day of their marriage.

0600 Hours
December 26, 1972
Patterson Residence
Married Officers Housing
Ft. Hood, TX

Chris unfolded the morning newspaper, the *Killeen Daily Herald*. Glaring at him from the front page, color pictures of Jackson and his men under the banner headline - **U.S. Army Traitors Escape Custody**. Talk about the press finding them guilty without the formality of a trial.

Blackwater, Carter, Roberts, and Mason's pictures were taken at the Ft. Bragg stockade. They were wearing faded OD-green jungle fatigues and had shaved heads. Chris recognized Jackson's picture in his class A uniform. It came from his promotion ceremony to Lt. Colonel in Vietnam. Why didn't they use the same intake picture as the others?

He read the article but it didn't make sense. The reporter wrote the men were armed with a Colt .45 caliber pistol and M16, obtained from the guards. According to regulations, there were no weapons other than nightsticks carried in the cell blocks. Only one thing rang true. They stole a car – a black four-door AMC 1969 Ambassador with North Carolina license plate – CF-5856. It's what he would do and how they disappeared so quickly.

Since the general gave the staff an extra day off for the Christmas holidays, Chris dressed in his fatigues and headed for the office. The commo room would be manned by a single soldier monitoring communications. Today, that traffic would be light.

With a swagger to his step, Chris entered the communications room.

The sergeant behind the counter snapped to attention. "Colonel, don't you have the day off?"

"Yes, but I need to see the log."

The man handed it over quickly. "Here, sir. I need to use the latrine. Could you watch the office for me?"

"Sure."

The man exited the room, whistling a snappy tune.

Chris found the records he wanted quickly. An APB-All Points Bulletin sent out by the 525th Military Intelligence Group – Ft. Bragg, NC. He could read it without anyone in the room.

12/24/72 – 0800 hours

To all law enforcement agencies - check medical facilities for a sick individual exhibiting symptoms of possible organ failure and jaundice within 500-1000 miles of Fort Bragg, NC.

Suspect #1: Lt. Colonel Jackson J. MacKenzie, United States Army - Race: White, Eyes: Blue, Height: 6'1", Weight: 125 pounds, Hair: Dark blond but currently shaved off. Identifying marks: Crisscrossing scars on his back, recent scar on right shoulder and thigh.

Four other individuals will possibly be with him. They are as follows:

Suspect #2: Captain William "Bill" L. Mason, United States Army - Race: White, Eyes: Brown, Height: 5'7", Weight: 160 pounds, Hair: Brown in a crew cut. Identifying marks: Dagger – "Death before Dishonor" tattoo on left forearm.

Suspect #3: 1st Lieutenant Tyler "Ty" M. Carter, United States Army - Race: White (can pass for ethnic with a dark, tanned complexion) Eyes: Brown, Height: 5' 10", Weight: 175 pounds, Hair: Dark brown, short and curly.

Suspect #4: Sergeant First Class Dakota "Chief" C. Blackwater, United States Army - Race: American Indian, Eyes: Brown, Height 6'2", Weight: 250 pounds, Hair: Black in a crew cut, Identifying marks: Bald Eagle tattoo on upper right shoulder.

Suspect #5: Staff Sergeant Michael "Mikey" P. Roberts, United States Army – Race: White, Eyes: Brown, Height: 5'9", Weight 150 pounds, Hair: Dark brown in a crew cut. Identifying marks: Scar on right calf.

These men escaped from the maximum-security area of the Fort Bragg stockade between 2000 hours on 12/23/72 and 0700 hours on 12/24/72. They are considered armed and extremely dangerous. Do not attempt to apprehend without backup. They are all trained United States Army Green Berets and experts in hand-to-hand combat, weapons, tactics and speak several different languages. SSGT Roberts is a medic, so also be on the lookout for break-ins or thefts from medical offices, pharmacies, and clinics. They may be driving a 1969 black 4-door AMC Ambassador with North Carolina license plate – CF-5856. If any of these men are spotted, contact the 525th Military Intelligence Group – Ft. Bragg, NC.

Chris put the report back in the file before the sergeant returned. He didn't find the APB much help either. It seemed full of misinformation as well. But what concerned him. The part about Jackson's health and weight – 125 pounds. Jackson, at six-foot-one, carried two hundred muscled-up pounds easily on his broad shouldered frame with room for more. If he was that thin, he was extremely sick. Not good at all.

CHAPTER 22

1900 Hours
March 29, 1973
Married Officers Housing
Patterson Residence
Ft. Hood, TX

Chris got up from his chair, walked to the wet bar and poured himself a full glass of the most expensive whiskey in the cabinet – Crown Royal. A Christmas gift from his executive officer.

Kara joined him as he took a long sip, snaking her arm across his back. "Chris, you promised. No more drinking."

"I know."

"Why?"

He pointed at the unfolded newspaper on the table next to his chair. The front-page headline. **US Withdraws from Vietnam**.

"Vietnam? The pullout today?" Kara asked. "We've known this date for two months."

"Yeah. We're finally out of that fucking God forsaken country."

"I won't ding you this time."

Chris realized he cursed in front of her. "I'm—"

She placed a finger on his lips. "Don't. I agree. You have every right to say that."

"Thanks." Chris kissed her finger. "I love you."

"Do you want to talk about it?"

He shook his head *no*, crossed the living room with his drink, and stood before his West Point class picture, wiping the dust off the glass with his sleeve. How many of them died in that awful place? Men like him and Jackson, shaped, injured, and changed mentally and physically by that endless war.

Unlike Korea, where he was proud to have fought, this conflict didn't have that same feeling. Too many innocents died, like those poor defenseless kids. Too many rules made by politicians looking out for their own interests who didn't give a damn. The soldiers, sailors, and Marines didn't have a chance to win, and the American public hated them.

Even though the U.S military won the battles, in the end, they lost the war. Something that stuck like a splintered chicken bone in the throat of a West Point graduate. They weren't trained to lose.

He raised his glass. "This one's for you guys, wherever you are."

Kara stood next to him with a small glass of whiskey. "Ditto. I hope Jackson's somewhere safe?"

"I'm sure he is." *Probably feeling just like me today. Sad. So many of us died for nothing.*

They held their glasses up for those who didn't come home.

0730 Hours
April 30, 1973
1st Cavalry Division Headquarters
8th Regiment
Ft. Hood, TX

As Chris walked through the outer doors on the way to his office, the clerk at the front desk whistled.

"Colonel, I have something for you," the sergeant said, holding out an envelope. "I was told to give it to you first thing."

"Thank you." Chris took the envelope. Typed on the front his name, rank, and duty station. No stamp or return address. It was an internal letter. Why not place it in his office? He continued on, unlocking his door and sitting behind his desk.

Before opening the envelope, he checked the messages in his inbox. Nothing important. A couple of men on sick call, one written up for insubordination, and one in the drunk tank after a weekend bender.

Leaning back in his chair, Chris opened the envelope and pulled out the letter.

DEPARTMENT OF THE ARMY
OFFICE OF THE COMMANDING OFFICER
1ST CAVALRY DIVISION
BUILDING 28000
FT. HOOD, TX 76544

29 April 1973

Lt. Colonel Christopher S. Patterson
1st Cavalry Division Headquarters
8th Regiment
Building 28000
Ft. Hood, TX 76544

Dear Lt. Colonel Patterson,

The FY73/74 Promotion Board recently reported out, and regretfully, you were not selected in this first of three looks. At this stage, your non-selection is not necessarily a negative reflection of your potential for command in a higher rank since only 20 percent of eligible candidates were selected.

You will compete against your promotion year group in two additional Command Screening Boards in the future. The next board is scheduled for April 1974 and will have a selection opportunity of approximately 30 percent. Should you fail to be selected by this board, you will compete one last time in either April 1975 or 1976, depending on the current needs of the U.S. Army. The total selection opportunity for Colonel over the three boards is approximately 75 percent for your promotion year group.

I encourage you to contact me should you have any questions regarding the screening process. Competition to achieve this critical career milestone will remain extremely competitive. Keep charging forward as one of The First Team.

You are being transferred to command the 27th Maintenance Battalion at Ft. Hood, effective immediately. Report to my clerk for your orders upon receipt of this memorandum. Please have your office moved by the end of the week.

Brigadier General Julius Crass
Commanding Officer
1st Cavalry Division

Chris wadded up the paper and tossed it into his trash can. He probably should have kept it for his personal records, but he couldn't stop himself. The first strike against his promotion to full Colonel.

There was nothing on his last eval to warrant being passed over. He couldn't figure out why. While he could appeal, he didn't see a point except to place another red flag in his records as a non-conformist. The general sent a standard form letter. He didn't want Chris to contact him. If the general wanted to talk to him, he wouldn't have sent a letter. As a West Point graduate, the general would have talked to him privately.

Maintenance wasn't his first choice, second, or even third. More like last. Chris would rather be commanding a tank or artillery unit with the 1st Cav moving into armor, something that went into combat, not relegated to a behind the lines maintenance battalion. He didn't know a thing about engines.

1400 Hours
May 5, 1974
1st Cavalry Division Headquarters
The 27th Maintenance Battalion Office
Ft. Hood, TX

The multi-line phone near the edge of his standard gray metal desk came to life with an obnoxious ring. Chris placed a signed report into his in-box, picked up the handset, pressed the blinking light, and put the receiver to his ear. "Lieutenant Colonel Patterson." Just saying it made him wince inside. The promotion board passed him over again last week.

"Colonel, you have a visitor," Sergeant Banaszek, his clerk said.

A visitor? No one ever visited him besides his wife or office staff to bring him more forms to sign. "Who?"

"A colonel. He didn't give his name, sir."

JAG? CID? "Send him in." Chris stood and straightened his fatigue shirt. Sweat dripped down his back. Was he in trouble? He'd find out soon.

The door opened, and a tall man entered the room wearing a class A uniform. A Combat Infantry Badge, the DSC, Silver Star, Soldiers Medal, Bronze Star, National Defense, Vietnam Service, and Vietnam Campaign ribbons adorned the left side of his jacket. Chris recognized him instantly. A classmate from West Point. He entertained them in the barracks with his guitar. "Scott...I mean Colonel Hannaford." He was glad Scott made it through Vietnam.

Hannaford shook his head. "Scott is fine, Chris. Let's not stand on formalities."

"Sit, please." Chris motioned at the chair in front of his desk. "What brings you to Fort Hood?"

Scott sat in the proffered chair and set his cover on the desktop. "Just on a layover on my way to Fort Campbell. Do I need a reason to visit a friend?" Scott asked.

Chris smiled. Something about Scott's demeanor seemed off, and that made him suspicious. Could someone have put him up to this? It felt more like a spot inspection than a visit. "No. But there has to be more to it than that." *Maybe he's here to offer me a position in his command. I'll take anything to escape this boring paper pushing, rubber stamping nonsense.*

"There is." Scott nodded at the office door. "How secure is this room?"

"As secure as a maintenance office can be." He hated saying maintenance. *What's going on? Does he think my office is bugged or something? Is it? Maybe he's warning me. Am I being watched?*

Scott went to the door, engaged the lock in the doorknob, and returned to his chair.

"Out with it, Scott," Chris demanded.

"I heard you got passed over for promotion again."

"I did. Stop stalling. That's not why you're here."

Scott pulled a newspaper clipping out of his jacket pocket then handed it to him. "This."

Chris unfolded the tattered piece of paper. He'd seen this article. It was the one sent out by the AP and UPI about Jackson's escape from the Ft. Bragg stockade. "You're here about MacKenzie?" Even though Scott was one of his oldest friends, he had to seem distant about the issue. He didn't want to tip his hand.

"Now, look who's stalling. Have you heard anything?"

"Only what's in the newspapers or Army dispatches. Why?"

Scott leaned forward and lowered his voice. "Because I don't believe a word of this...bullshit."

Is he playing me or really in Jackson's corner? Chris placed the article on his desk and leaned back in his chair. "Why is that?"

"It's not in his nature, and you know it!" Scott banged his fist on the desk. "What's up with you? Why'd you call him MacKenzie, not Jackson or JJ?"

Chris straightened in his chair but didn't answer.

"You don't trust me," Scott said in an annoyed air.

"I don't know where you stand."

"Do you mean about who's side I'm on? The Army or Jackson's."

Chris nodded. "Yes."

"I figured you of all people would know. Maybe I was wrong to come here." Scott stood, shaking his head.

Chris studied Scott's expression. He seemed distressed and disappointed by Chris' indifference. As Scott reached for his cover, Chris placed his hand on it. "Stop. Please sit down."

Scott studied him for a moment. "You were testing me?"

"Yes. You know as well as I do discussing Jackson's situation openly is not kosher. That's why you locked the door."

"I sure do. Now, what do you know."

"Probably the same things as you." Chris held up the newspaper article. "The stuff in the news reports and dispatches. None of it adds up."

"My thoughts too. Jackson normally weighs two hundred pounds, not one twenty-five. I'm worried about his health."

Scott caught the weight and health issue too. "So am I."

"What can we do about it?"

"Nothing until they either catch him."

"Not possible," Scott interjected. "He's too smart to allow that to happen again."

Chris smiled. He knew that as well. "Or he comes forward on his own. I see that the more likely option when he finds what he needs to clear his name. All we can do is wait." He was glad Jackson still had friends who believed in him. And he wasn't alone in his belief of Jackson's innocence.

Scott checked his watch then pushed himself out of his chair. "I have to get to the airfield. My plane leaves in an hour."

"Before you leave." Chris opened the bottom drawer of his desk and pulled out a bottle of scotch and two glasses. It was always good to have a bottle on hand, even against the regs. If a superior wanted a drink, he was prepared. He poured two fingers into each glass. Kara didn't need to know. He'd just have one drink. It was a special occasion. He didn't see his classmates very often.

Scott picked up one glass and Chris the other.

"To absent friends, alive and dead," Chris said.

They clinked the glasses together.

1730 Hours
April 30, 1975
Married Officers Housing
Patterson Residence
Ft. Hood, TX.

Sitting on their living room couch, Chris and Kara sat glued to the television. On the screen, Dan Rather of the CBS Evening News.

"South Vietnam now is under communist control," Rather said in an emotionless monotone. "Early today, beginning with a jeep load of rather rag-tag Viet Cong soldiers then truck after truck of heavily armed North Vietnamese regular troops, the communists entered Saigon in force. South Vietnamese President Dương Văn Minh, just two days in office, surrendered his government unconditionally. His whereabouts are not known. The surrender came just four hours after the last Americans were pulled out of Saigon."

Chris shook his head at the images behind the news anchor taken yesterday during the embassy evacuation. The various aircraft ranged from UH-1 "Huey" helicopters, the saviors of the grunt, tandem-rotor Chinooks, Sikorsky Jolly Green Giants, to C-130 transports and fighter/bombers.

They flew around in an endless menagerie picking up Americans and those South Vietnamese lucky enough to grab a seat. The rest were left to the auspices of North Vietnam. Anyone associated with the United States wouldn't live long.

Kara gripped his hand as the interviews continued, Ed Bradley in Manila after escaping from Saigon and the correspondents standing on the White House lawn talking about President Ford and former President Nixon.

The entire thing seemed surreal as the broadcast continued. Chris didn't know how to put his emotions into context except to feel rage and anger. Over 50,000 Americans died over there for nothing to watch the South Vietnamese government give up without a whimper. Those members of the South Vietnamese military that couldn't escape were removing their uniforms to avoid capture and death.

Kara tapped him on the shoulder. So caught up in his emotions, he didn't realize she'd let go of his hand or got up. He looked over as she pressed a full glass of ice and whiskey into his palm.

"Take this," she said.

"Are you sure?" he asked, wondering if he should drink it. He hadn't taken a drink in two years. Was she testing him?

"Yes, today you have my permission. Moderation, remember." She held up a similar glass. "I'm joining you. Tell me what you're feeling."

How did he put it into words? "I can't explain it." His emotions felt like an erupting volcano spewing lava everywhere. He was all over the map.

"Give me one word. Be honest."

Chris banged his fist on his leg several times. He needed the pain to think. "Frustrated." Then the words poured out. "Betrayed by the politicians. Angry they wouldn't let us win. Their rules of engagement got my men killed. There were days we couldn't shoot back. I'm not talking about not having ammo or supplies either."

"I don't understand," Kara said.

"We fought the war with one arm tied behind our backs. The rules of engagement dictated when we could fight Charlie. We could attack only if attacked first." He wanted to laugh at this one. "Did you know there is a Michelin rubber tree plantation near Saigon that maintained operations during the war?"

"No." Kara gripped his shoulder. "What's that mean?"

"We couldn't call in artillery strikes within the plantation when Charlie set up positions inside its borders. If those trees were damaged in any way, the US had to compensate Michelin for the losses." Chris rolled his eyes. "So don't shoot the trees."

Kara looked surprised. "Really?"

"Yeah. We had to clear the plantation by hand. Men died to save trees."

"Oh my God!"

"Money talks. The politicians had no idea what the mission was in Vietnam other than protecting their careers. What was our goal other than prop up the South Vietnamese government? I still don't know. A two-year-old could draw up a better battle plan with crayons and a coloring book."

Kara chuckled. "I can just picture that."

Chris nodded. "We answered our nation's call and defended the Constitution. Our freedom. And the politicians stabbed us in the back. We didn't want to be in that shithole of a country. We just wanted to come home alive. Many didn't. They came home on ice inside a fucking body bag." He realized what he had said. "I'm sorry."

Kara gripped his hand. "Don't be. I completely understand. I feel the same as you. Disgusted."

"Thanks." He sipped his drink. Warmth spread down his throat into his stomach. What did he have to show for his three years in hell? A drinking problem he fought with every day, a broken friendship, a civilian public that didn't understand, nightmares of dead kids, and the memories of the men he lost in battle. Not a fair trade.

CHAPTER 23

1000 Hours
January 2, 1976
1st Cavalry Division Headquarters
The 27th Maintenance Battalion Office
Ft. Hood, TX

Up to his neck in paperwork and tired of reading maintenance reports of the battalion's sub-units, Chris shoved them aside and got up to look out the window. He watched the wind blow the distant trees under the yellow-red sun as it moved east to west across the blue sky.

All he did was sit behind a desk and sign his name. He hated his duties. Supervise, establish priorities, assign duties, establish maintenance program guidelines, advise and assist in planning, advise brigade of all maintenance, obtain parts, repair support, assess problems, recommend solutions, and anticipate brigade requirements. He was an infantry soldier, not a mechanic or a damn file clerk.

Begrudgingly, he returned to his desk. These reports were due in the brigade office with his signature by the end of the business day.

His desk phone rang next to his right hand. He set his pen on the desktop, pressed the blinking button for the incoming call, and picked up the receiver. "Lieutenant Colonel Patterson speaking."

"Sir, General Benedict is here to see you," Sergeant Banaszek, his clerk said.

"Send him in." Chris hung up and stood, straightening his green fatigues shirt then wiping a quick hand across his head to smooth down any loose hairs.

The general entered the office, surprisingly wearing green fatigues, and acknowledged Chris with a nod. "Lieutenant Colonel Patterson."

"Please sit, General." Chris pointed at his padded rolling chair.

"No, it's yours but thank you." General Benedict removed the folder from under his arm and sat in the straight-backed wooden chair in front of the desk.

Chris sat carefully in his chair. He didn't want it to scoot out from under him and make him look like a fool if he missed. "To what do I owe the pleasure, sir?" He hadn't met the general yet, even though he took command of the division last year. Not usual, but not normal either for the division commander not to introduce himself to a battalion commander, even one over maintenance. If the tanks, jeeps, and trucks don't work correctly, that's a problem.

"I'm here to make you an offer. One authorized by the Chief of Staff."

That piqued Chris' interest. Anything was better than this duty station. "What, sir?"

"Let me start with this. You've been passed over for promotion to Colonel twice in the last three years, correct?"

"Yes, sir." Something Chris didn't understand unless the orphanage was still hanging over his head. Or maybe his former relationship with Jackson. The boards never tell you why. His eval scores had always been well above average.

"That puts you in a terminal rank of Lieutenant Colonel. What General George Marshall called 'dead wood.'"

"Yes, sir." *Where's he going with this?*

The general placed the folder on the desk and pushed it across to Chris. "Take a look."

Chris opened the folder. On the top page, dated today, was a promotion order to full Colonel with his name on it, signed by the new Army Chief of Staff, General Coffey. "You called this an offer, sir. What do I have to do to make it happen?" If he didn't, with two strikes against him, he could be forced into retirement as early as next year on June 4th, the anniversary date of his West Point graduation.

"Turn the page."

Chris did as instructed. He hadn't already because he didn't want to steal the general's thunder in telling him. Staff officers loved to keep you in suspense.

The next page was an undated transfer order with his name and the rank of Colonel to the 902nd Military Intelligence Group at Fort Meade. It was a huge step up from maintenance. Kara would love a change of scenery to Maryland. But the posting had him confused. Intel wasn't in his bailiwick. Not even close.

"Can I ask why, sir?" Chris asked.

"Keep turning."

On the next page was an intelligence report, dated 20 April 1975.

To all US military installations in the United States:

Subject: Lt. Colonel MacKenzie, US Army, 5th Special Forces Group - AWOL

On 12 April 1975, Lieutenant Colonel Jackson J. MacKenzie, Captain William L. Mason, 1st Lieutenant Tyler M. Carter, Sergeant First Class Dakota C. Blackwater, and Staff Sergeant Michael P. Roberts are rumored to have taken an active part in the evacuation of the Cambodian embassy. The 902nd Military Intelligence Group is working on corroboration of this action. An unknown sixth individual also took part, who could, through the physical description, be Major Harrison Russell, U.S. Army, retired.

Staff Sergeant Michael P. Roberts has been confirmed KIA during the extraction and buried in his hometown, Garden City, KS, on 17 April 1975. Colonel Hammond attempted to speak to his parents, but he left without obtaining any information. Hammond also attempted to speak with Major Russell at his residence in San Clemente, CA, to determine if he was involved. No information was obtained, and a subsequent federal contempt of court complaint was filed due to the court order in effect stating that Army personnel are not to go within one hundred yards of the Russell household.

Updates will be forwarded as received as this is still a highly sensitive political matter. Information regarding this case has been deemed – Classified – Need to know – Eyes only. Do not forward this information to the press.

Pentagon
General Windom
U.S. Army Chief of Staff

Now Chris was confused. He had been stonewalled every time he tried to obtain information about Jackson. He had to scratch and claw in order to find out what little he did know. Then it hit him, the new rank, the transfer. And he didn't like the idea one bit. "You want me to find MacKenzie?"

General Benedict nodded. "Yes. Of all the people in the Army, as his roommate at the academy, you know him best. I bet you shared a lot with each other."

"We did, sir. But his parents are dead. So is his older brother. He died in Vietnam as a Navy SEAL. MacKenzie has no ties other than his Army ones. How am I supposed to locate him?"

"Think back on your past, Colonel Patterson. I'm sure the information is there somewhere. Along with the promotion and assignment, your security clearance is upgraded to top-secret with limited privileges for certain sensitive compartmentalized information. You now have access to all information regarding..." The general paused. "The traitor, MacKenzie," he spat venomously.

Chris wanted to say Jackson wasn't a traitor but didn't. "And if I refuse, sir?" This felt like a betrayal to all the things Jackson confided in him at West Point. Other than his men, Jackson was alone. He knew things Jackson told no one else. And that's why the Army was using him. Pathetic and dishonorable. Not the ideals taught at the academy.

"If you refuse...well, it's in your best interest not to, but if you do, keep counting engines and motor oil until you and your wife end up on the breadline...in a little over a year. We're in the middle of a recession. Is that how you want to attend your West Point Black '57 twentieth reunion? Dead wood. Retired? On welfare."

Of all the decisions he had to make in his life, this was the hardest. Betray his friend...former friend and right the sinking ship on his career? He had a feeling what happened between them had more to do with their internal demons than hatred, and they were both drunk. A dangerous combination to friendship.

General Benedict started tapping his foot. "I need an answer, Patterson! I don't have all day."

"Yes," slipped out of Chris' mouth without thinking.

"Would you like to know why the promotion board skipped you over twice? With your evaluation scores, awards, and battle record, you should've made it on the first try. It wasn't just the orphanage."

That sounded ominous. "Why, sir?"

"Because you couldn't keep your fool ass nose out of the MacKenzie business. Do you think we didn't notice the unauthorized trips into the commo room? Or the off the books phone calls? We even know about Colonel Hannaford's visit. When Hammond got shipped off to Fort Wainwright in Alaska for being stupid, the new Chief of Staff figured if we couldn't control your curiosity, we'd use it to our advantage."

"Yes, sir." *Shit, they knew. I hope Scott is okay.*

"Consider yourself lucky, Colonel Patterson, that you're not taking up residence in MacKenzie's old cell for conduct unbecoming. Start packing. That transfer becomes effective one week from today. You have another week from that point to report in at Fort Meade and get to work."

"Yes, sir." *They mean business.* How would he explain this to his wife? He'd tell Kara this way he could help Jackson by finding out what happened. If he ever located him, keep him from being killed. Deadly force had been authorized in their capture if the men resisted. What worried him, if that happened, Kara would never forgive him.

1900 Hours
Married Officers Housing
Patterson Residence
Ft. Hood, TX

Figuring after dinner was the best time to tell Kara, he waited until they both sat on the living room couch to watch TV. "I'm being promoted and transferred to Maryland."

"That's wonderful. I've never been to Maryland." Kara beamed from ear to ear. "But you told me after they bypassed you the last time, you're probably headed toward retirement." She cocked her head. "Why did they change their minds?"

Chris handed her the packet General Benedict gave him. "Read this."

Kara thumbed through the paperwork. "They want you to do what? Catch Jackson. That's the reason for your promotion and us moving to Maryland?" Kara handed everything back to him and crossed her arms. Her flushed face, pursed lips, and stiff posture told of her anger.

"Yes. I—"

"Didn't have a choice because of your career. So what if they retire you next year. You'd have a great pension to fall back on. You're young enough to find something else and do another twenty years. With your engineering degree from West Point, you could get a job anywhere and make a hell of a lot more money. We could get our own house and a newer car. Maybe even a new one."

Chris shrugged. "I know, but I don't want to retire yet."

Kara stomped her foot. "And finding Jackson, your friend since West Point and mine since elementary school, is the only way to keep your precious career going?"

"Yeah, because—"

She interrupted him again. "You're going to help him by throwing him back into prison? We both know that didn't work out well the last time. Did you ever stop to consider what I might think about this?"

She got him. He didn't. "No. I thought you'd be all for it," Chris said.

"That's where you went wrong."

"But the general needed an answer right then, and I gave him one."

"And like a good, obedient little soldier, you said yes."

That quip stung Chris' ego like a jellyfish. "Yeah. It slipped out."

Kara tapped his shirt collar. "Can you decline the promotion?"

"Technically, yes. There's some paperwork involved and hoops to jump through." Chris enveloped her hand in his. "Why would I want to?"

Kara pulled her hand away. "You need to think about that answer before I give it to you." She got up, ran to the bedroom, and slammed the door.

Chris didn't understand what she meant. Why was she so angry at him? He stood, went to their bedroom door, and knocked gently. "Can I come in?"

"No," came Kara's raised voice through the door.

Sighing, Chris returned to the living room and poured himself a glass of scotch at the wet bar. Before taking a drink, he stared at their wedding picture on the wall. She looked so beautiful standing next to him. Her long white dress glowed against his dress blue uniform.

Did he make a huge mistake by not asking the general for time to discuss it with his wife? Was his marriage in jeopardy? Could CID know about Kara's connection to Jackson and want to use it through him?

Chris swirled the scotch around in the glass, watching the tiny gold tornado appear then disappear. A funnel-shaped vortex in fluid dynamics going nowhere. He set the glass down, returned to the bedroom door, and knocked again. "Can I come in?"

"Go ahead," Kara called out.

"Thanks." Chris slowly swung the door open. He didn't want to get hit by any outgoing missiles like shoes or something harder. Kara was sitting on their bed, blotting her eyes with a tissue. He walked over and sat next to her, running a thumb across her damp cheek. "I'm sorry. But I don't understand. I know he's your friend but why's Jackson so special to you? What does it matter if I take the job?"

Kara gave him a half-smile. "I've never told you this. It's easy to find if you know where to look. Jackson's father saved my dad on Okinawa. He was wounded at Mount Yaetake. Major MacKenzie defended an aid station full of injured Marines from a banzai charge with a box of grenades and a Thompson."

"And one of them was your dad."

"Yes." Kara gripped Chris' hand. "His father protected mine. Jackson, wherever he is, has no one to protect him. His family is dead. All he had was his career. That was his dream. Just like yours."

"You read the intelligence report. He's fine." *I wonder how long it took him to get that way?*

"You know what I mean. The Army is vilifying him in each press release like he's the devil's spawn. The fact they sought you out says they're desperate to find him."

"You want me to protect him? Honey, I can't. You know we had a falling out. After what I did, he probably hates me. While I know some of that fight was my fault, he did throw the first punch."

"And that says something was eating at him from the inside, just like you with the memories of those kids. You're both at fault. Does that mean you have to kick him in the teeth too?"

"No. Do you want me to take the job or not?"

"Take it, and we'll move to Maryland. At least with you, he'll have a chance and someone who will listen, unlike that fat-ass Colonel Hammond, who wanted to put him into the ground." Kara grabbed his hands. "Please don't shoot Jackson."

Chris looped his arm around her shoulders. "Only if I have to…but knowing him, he won't hurt me unless he's boxed in with no way out."

"Then don't box him in. Always give him an exit route. The Army doesn't have to know." She laughed. "Call it job security until you decide to retire."

"Hmmm." Chris thought about it for a moment. She did have a point, and he wanted to save his marriage. If he didn't agree, she might divorce him. He'd probably never catch Jackson. The man could outthink the legendary All-Seeing Eye. "Agreed."

Kara kissed his cheek. "Then we'd better start packing up the house."

Chris stood and pulled her into his arms. "Yes, ma'am, Mrs. Patterson."

CHAPTER 24

0800 Hours
January 18, 1976
Building 54 - Nathan Hale Hall
902nd Military Intelligence Group Headquarters
"The Deuce"
Ft. Meade, MD

Chris parked his Army-issued green sedan in the parking lot near the four-story World War II era red brick building. Today he took command but without a change of command ceremony. He didn't want one. Finding Jackson wasn't the only duty of the 902nd MI. Only he and his aide were tasked with that assignment due to security concerns.

The 902nd MI was the spearpoint to protecting the United States in the Cold War against the communist regimes. It conducted counterintelligence support for the U.S. Army and other commands with detachments in multiple locations both in and out of the United States. The cold war with the Soviet Union kept them busy tracking agents, possible espionage, nuclear weapons, and hot spots around the globe.

He liked the new left shoulder patch of the 902nd MI on his green class A dress uniform. The patch had an oriental blue half globe on the bottom with a gold Sphinx projected against a black background on top. An upright dagger joined both halves. The Sphinx and oriental blue color represented Military Intelligence.

The night before, Kara had sewn the 1st Cavalry patch on the right shoulder of his jacket, replacing the 3rd Infantry as his combat patch so he'd be ready for today. One thing was hard for him, removing the crossed sabers of the cavalry on his jacket lapels and replacing them with a new branch insignia. A gold dagger - point up, under a gold sun with four straight and four wavy alternating rays surmounted on a gold rose, the petals made of dark blue enamel.

The sun represented Helios, who could see and hear everything. The straight rays were the four points of the compass. The rose was an ancient symbol of secrecy. And the partially concealed, unsheathed dagger showed the aggressive, protective requirements and the physical danger inherent in their mission. Now he was one of the guys he and everyone else complained about in Vietnam. The guys with MI never got anything right. What intelligence?

Chris nodded at the personnel manning the lobby and took the stairs to his office. The four-story climb allowed him to think. Was this really what he wanted? His only answer, yes, unless he wanted to pump gas at the local filling station.

He opened the door to the office with his name and rank properly painted on the door. It was a long way from a piece of masking tape like he had in 'Nam. Since he had to project an image of authority, he asked his new aide, 2nd Lieutenant Carlos Ortiz, to hang his framed awards and newly shadow-box-mounted West Point Firstie sword in his office.

Upon meeting Ortiz, Chris realized the young man had potential. A college football player, a linebacker, voted captain of the defense his senior year. He graduated with honors from UCLA then top of his class at Officers Candidate School. The kid had only one flaw. He was green as the grass outside and needed a lot of seasoning. Something he wouldn't get in intelligence. His inexperience was probably why some numskull officer in the base personnel department assigned him as Chris' aide. Whether that was by design or a joke Chris didn't know yet.

Everything in the office looked perfect. A new desk and padded rolling chair were stationed near a bookcase and a file cabinet. In the corners sat flagpoles bearing the colors of the 902nd MI and the American flag. His awards and shadow box were spaced nicely on the wood-paneled walls. A table with a steaming coffee pot, a container of non-dairy creamer, sugar packets, plastic stirrers, and Styrofoam cups

What didn't look perfect, the brown cardboard storage boxes stacked in date order next to his desk at nearly waist level. All the reports that had anything to do with Jackson since the escape in 1972, plus his service record book. He requested the daily guard reports and Jackson's medical records from Ft. Bragg. Those he couldn't get. The reply…not needed for his assignment, and that all-important word – *classified* above your clearance level. He had a top-secret clearance with an SCI add-on. That meant something was in them the brass didn't want him to see. Otherwise, why would medical records be classified?

Chris set his briefcase next to the desk, opened the lid of the top box, and pulled out a thick brown folder – Jackson's service record book. He placed that on his desk. The paper on top of the stack underneath was the APB-All Points Bulletin sent out by the 525th Military Intelligence Group at Ft. Bragg, NC, on 12/24/72. This one he'd already seen. He flipped it upside down on his desk and placed the box beside it.

After settling into his chair, he picked up the next page to read.

To: US Army Criminal Investigations Command

From: INTERPOL General Secretariat – Red Notice

We have received information that two AWOL members of the United States Army were possibly involved in a murder on French soil on 05 April 1973. The shooter (suspect 1) was possibly Lt. Colonel MacKenzie, Jackson J. The spotter (suspect 2) was possibly Captain Mason, William L. Killed was the Mayor of Saint-Jean-de-Luz. We believe they were paid a half million US dollars for the hit by an opposition candidate.

Description as follows:
Suspect 1 – 5'10" – 6'0", Weight: 225 pounds, Hair: Brown/crew cut
Suspect 2 – 5'09 – 5'10". Weight: 190 pounds, Hair: Brown/crew cut

He flipped that load of bullshit over. Jackson wasn't a cold-blooded killer. The weight, height, hair color, and style didn't match either. The Army wanted to pin a bogus charge on him. With this many reports to read, he had a lot of catching up to do. And a few pots of coffee to consume.

To calm down, he picked up Jackson's SRB. He knew most of what was inside. Jackson's accomplishments as both an enlisted man in the Korean War and later an officer after graduating from West Point were extensive and impressive. Blue Infantry cord, Special Forces qualified, Second award Combat Infantry Badge, Combat Medic Badge, Senior Aviator Wings, Master Combat Parachutist wings, Master Freefall Parachutist badge, Rigger, and the EOD badge.

His list of medals told an even greater story of his bravery in two wars: Medal of Honor, DSC with bronze oak leaf cluster, DSM, Silver Star with oak leaf cluster, Legion of Merit, DFC with V device, Soldier's Medal, Bronze Star with V device and an oak leaf cluster, Purple Heart with a silver oak leaf cluster. Air Medal with V device, Joint Services Commendation with V device, Army Commendation with V device, National Defense with a bronze star, Korean Service with two bronze battle stars, Armed Forces Expeditionary with a bronze star and arrowhead. Vietnam Service with an arrowhead and silver battle star, Republic of Vietnam Gallantry Cross with Palm, Republic of Vietnam Armed Forces 1C Honor Medal, UN Korean Service Ribbon, and Republic of Vietnam Campaign Ribbon.

And one not approved for wear - The Republic of Korea War Service Medal, but Jackson did anyway. His small rebellion against the rules and regulations. He served there.

Chris agreed. He wore his too.

It was inconceivable as to why anyone would want to screw over someone with a service record like Jackson's. Chris needed to look at those records to get the bad taste out of his mouth after seeing with the Interpol Red Notice what a malicious attack the Army was doing to Jackson's reputation. From hero to zero. Medal of Honor recipient to traitor. Hopefully, he wouldn't be joining him.

1200 Hours
April 10, 1976
Valley View Cemetery
Garden City, KS

As Chris walked across the greening grass through the rows of gravestones, he thought about the one thing that brought him to Kansas. He needed to know. Were Jackson and his men involved with the evacuation of the Cambodian Embassy? The official word from the Army was *no*. However, the State Department personnel they saved told him a different story. If nothing else, he had to do this. That's why he wore his class A uniform.

Following the instructions from the funeral home, he found the white marble military headstone quickly. It stood out gleaming in the bright sunlight of a cloudless Kansas afternoon. He stepped around to the front and looked at the inscription under the Christian cross. *Michael Paul Roberts – Staff Sergeant U.S. Army - Bronze Star, Purple Heart, Meritorious Service Medal – Vietnam – Beloved Son – 10/26/45 – 04/12/75.*

He placed a fresh bouquet of multicolored flowers into the vase next to the stone. Lined up at its base, five moss-covered quarters. Other coins were scattered around the grave, some on the rounded top of the headstone. Pennies, nickels, a few dimes. Pennies meant a fellow serviceman or woman stopped by to pay their respects. Nickels showed the giver attended basic or other training with the deceased. A dime showed the visitor served with the decedent in some capacity.

But the quarters stood out. They meant the service member was with the person when they died. Those coins could only come from Jackson, Mason, Carter, Blackwater, and probably Russell, or whoever was the other person. The newspaper pictures did show six pallbearers in uniform. Five of them were in Army class As. One of those men was Russell. He gave the alibi he came because he learned Roberts died. However, there was another man, his face obscured by the others, wearing a dress blue Marine uniform with sergeant major stripes. The caption said, "unknown."

From the local newspaper pictures and the article about the ceremony, Jackson made sure to give Roberts a full military funeral with all the trappings. A twenty-one-gun salute from the VFW. Flag folding. Taps. Good for him.

Chris left a dime for his own reasons, knelt next to the headstone, said a silent prayer, crossed himself, and stood. Then he saluted the grave. The honor of one soldier to another who gave his life in service to his country. Saving those people merited the salute. He wished he could've been there unofficially for the ceremony.

1300 Hours
Outside of Garden City, KS

The Roberts farm wasn't overly large, but it wasn't small either. Acres of growing wheat fields stood on either side of the one-story white clapboard farmhouse with a covered wrap-around porch. The green metal rocking chairs made it look like the house jumped from a 1950s postcard. Beside the house was a red with white trim equipment barn. In front of the barn sat a green John Deere combine.

Chris parked his rental car in the driveway next to a woody station wagon. He hated coming here so close to the first anniversary of Michael Roberts' death. Who knew what reception he would get – friendly or confrontational?

Slowly he got out, straightened his class A uniform jacket, and walked up the sidewalk. Before he arrived at the door, it swung open, slamming against the wall with a loud bang, causing him to jump back.

At the threshold stood an older man, brown hair, five-nine, slim build, wearing jeans, work boots, and a white t-shirt. What stood out was the pump shotgun held crossways against his chest. Probably Michael Roberts' father.

"What are you doing here? We have a court order!" The man racked the shotgun for emphasis.

Chris held up his hands, taking a few steps back. This was unexpected. "I'm just here to talk."

"Hammond's done all the talking I want to hear."

Fucking Hammond, of course. "I'm not Hammond."

The man pointed the shotgun muzzle at Chris' chest. "I can see that."

Chris saw his life pass before his eyes. That muzzle bore looked a lot larger than a twelve gauge. He expected to die in combat, not visiting a wheat farm in Kansas. Hammond must have really screwed with the Roberts for him to get this kind of reception. "I know about the court order. I only want to talk to you. Are you Mr. Roberts?"

"Who else would I be? This is my house."

"Is your wife here?"

"Yes."

"Would it be possible to speak with you both...without the shotgun...please?"

Mr. Roberts lowered the shotgun muzzle. "Hammond never said please."

"Like I said." Chris pointed at himself. "I'm not Hammond. How'd you know I was coming?"

"The manager at the cemetery called me. Stay right where you are." Mr. Roberts ducked back into the house.

Chris stayed in place. He didn't want to get shot. Then he noticed the gold star hung in the front window and swallowed. What was about to happen?

Mr. Roberts returned without the shotgun. "Again, why are you here?"

"I want to know how your son died."

"You mean on the mission the Army says didn't happen."

"Yes." Chris decided to use his trump card. He pulled a picture of himself and Jackson in their West Point gray swallowtailed coats, white pants, red sash, and Firstie swords from his jacket pocket and handed it to Mr. Roberts.

Mr. Roberts looked from the picture to Chris then back at the picture. "That's Jackson. God, he's young. The other kid is you."

Chris smiled. "Yes. My name is Chris Patterson. JJ was my West Point roommate and oldest friend. We had a falling out in 'Nam over things we both had no control over. I still consider him part of me."

"I'm guessing you took over for Hammond."

"I did. He got transferred to Alaska."

"Good place for the—" Mr. Roberts glanced behind him then back to Chris. "Fucking asshole."

Agreed. His wife is like mine. Hates to hear him curse. "Sure is."

Mr. Roberts waved him forward. "Come on in."

Chris entered the house, removed his cover, and tucked it under his arm. In the entry hall stood an older woman with her gray hair in a bun and wearing a white apron over a blue dress.

Mr. Roberts handed her the picture. Just like her husband, she looked at the picture then at him.

"I'm Denise Roberts," she said. "You've already met my husband, Glen."

"Yes, ma'am."

"I heard you say you were Jackson's West Point roommate." She handed him the picture.

"Yes, ma'am."

"You even sound like him with the ma'am stuff. Call me Mrs. Roberts."

Chris chuckled as he returned the picture to his pocket. Jackson obviously made the same mistake and got the same short lecture. "Yes, Mrs. Roberts."

He followed them into the living room. They sat on the brown couch. To look at them, he sat directly across in an overstuffed blue fabric chair. Curious, he glanced around. On the fireplace mantel sat a triangular wooden flag case. Visible behind the glass were white stars on a field of blue. The case probably held their son's casket flag.

Around the case were framed photographs. One was of Michael Roberts in a class A uniform. Another picture was of Jackson sitting on a red horse with a white blaze and four socks. In front of him, the others stood encircled by a lasso.

The following picture was Michael Roberts and Jackson dressed in light blue hospital pajamas. Both men had shaved heads. Roberts looked decent. Jackson looked like death, a thin pale corpse in an extra-large potato sack. After the POW camp, maybe?

Still another was a group picture. The six men were wearing different college sweatshirts. Kansas Jayhawks, West Point, The Citadel, The University of Oklahoma, and The University of Indiana. The last picture was a smiling Michael Roberts in a tan Carhartt jacket.

Mr. Roberts leaned forward with his elbows on his knees. "What are your intentions, Colonel Patterson, since you're studying those pictures closely?"

He noticed. "I want to find out the truth."

"The real truth or the Army's version?"

"The truth, sir. No matter where it leads."

"That's a first," Mr. Roberts said sarcastically.

"And I understand your reservations." Chris took a chance. He needed to gain a rapport with them. A connection. "I know you lost your only child. I know how that feels. Right before I shipped out for 'Nam in '69, my daughter was born. She lived for less than a minute. The cord prolapsed around her neck at birth. We named her Amanda Elizabeth. My wife can't have any more children, and DHS didn't like me. Even though I was cleared, they used what happened at that orphanage against me."

"You're that Patterson!" Mrs. Roberts exclaimed.

"Yes, Mrs. Roberts. We got bad intel. I didn't know about the children. My men were dying around me. I ran out of options and used everything I had to save them. It still eats at me making that decision. But I'd do it again to save my men."

"Understandable," Mr. Roberts said. "We're sorry about your daughter."

"Me too," Chris said.

"Did you know my son wanted to become a doctor? That's why he became a combat medic."

Chris nodded. "As a matter of fact, I do. He told me." This he had to tell them. Even the U.S. Army hadn't picked up on it. Yet. It's why he left the dime. "During my first tour in 'Nam, I was with the 82nd Airborne. I was at the 95th Evac hospital visiting a friend the day it got zapped and came into contact with your son."

"Really?" Mrs. Roberts said.

"Yes. I ran across the compound and covered him with my rifle as he worked on the two men he saved in the bombing. I'm one of the officers who put him in for the Army Commendation Medal with Valor device. He sure showed it that day. Insisted I call him Mikey. I just want to know what happened to your son. I feel I owe him that."

"All his friends call him Mikey. I won't tell you where Jackson and the others are, but okay," Mr. Roberts said.

His friends? "That's fine, sir. I figured that. I wasn't going to ask." *I don't want to know. That means I'd have to go arrest them and maybe break the promise to my wife.*

"Mr. Roberts pointed at the flag then dropped his hand. "The CIA, calling themselves the State Department, contacted Jackson through an intermediary about members of the State Department staff stuck in a Buddhist monastery outside of Phnom Penh. When the embassy evacuation started, Jackson flew a Huey over the Thailand/Cambodian border to rescue them. During the extraction, one man went down. Michael ran out to save him but got hit in the stomach. Jackson flew everyone out to a carrier, but the Navy docs couldn't save Michael. Too much damage. Jackson flew Michael home, and we had the funeral. Jackson and the others left the next day."

Chris sighed, trying hard to hold in his emotions in front of the Roberts. Now he knew. Michael Roberts gave his life to save a stranger. "Thank you for telling me."

"You're welcome. Since you're Jackson's friend, did you know he was hit too?"

"How bad?" He didn't know that. It wasn't in any report he'd read. But that was consistent with the Army's reports about Jackson, completely wrong and full of misinformation.

"A round went through his left bicep. He looked horrible when that plane landed. He passed out in my car after flying here in considerable pain and over twenty-four hours with no sleep. The next day, he was a lot perkier and looked a damn sight better."

"That sounds like him. He's got the constitution of a mule."

"An Army one," Mr. Roberts kidded. "Isn't that the West Point mascot?"

Chris laughed. "It is." *He's right. Black, gray, and gold through and through.*

Mrs. Roberts handed her husband a piece of paper inside a frame. He, in turn, held it out to Chris.

"You might be interested in this," Mr. Roberts said.

The words told him more than the short version of the story from Mr. Roberts.

Dear Mr. and Mrs. Roberts,

I want to express our regret on the loss of your son, Staff Sergeant Michael Patrick Roberts, United States Army. He gave his life trying to save my senior aide, Calvin Freeman. Your son displayed tremendous character and bravery that day. In my heart, having met him for only a brief few minutes, Michael Roberts would have become one of this country's leading physicians. Grant yourself the time to grieve. Give thanks for the lives he saved.

As you comprehend this profound loss, let yourself cry, knowing each tear is a note of love rising to the heavens. - Author Unknown.

Robert Lincoln,
State Department
Deputy Chief of Mission - Cambodia

Chris handed the note back to Mr. Roberts. Now he remembered seeing those words in one of the newspaper articles. The brass wanted to burn every copy of that note. Freedom of the press gave them severe heartburn. "Thank you for your time."

"Would you like to stay for dinner?" Mrs. Roberts asked. "We'd love to have you stay and learn about all your West Point adventures with Jackson."

And he'd love to tell them but not now. "Maybe another time, m…Mrs. Roberts." He almost got her ire. "I have to get back."

"Where?" she asked.

"Maryland. Since I got back from 'Nam, I feel guilty even spending a few days away from my wife." He needed her. Seeing their stricken expressions as Mr. Roberts told him what happened ate at his soul. Michael Roberts was another young man with the potential to do great things lost to the hazards of war and politics.

2000 Hours
Garden City VFW Hall
1101 W. Mary Street
Garden City, KS

With it being Friday night, the asphalt parking lot was packed. The pouring rain on the roof of his car sounded like a thousand horses galloping on a brick road. Chris came here since he had time to kill with his flight canceled due to the weather. He'd changed into civilian clothes at the terminal to keep anyone from identifying him as Army Intelligence.

He could barely see the VFW meeting hall through the wall of water. A prefab rectangular faded red metal building. Part of the hall contained a bar. That's why he came. Maybe he could talk to someone with the same wartime experiences. Things he couldn't tell his wife. Ever.

Flipping the collar of his light jacket up around his ears and placing a newspaper over his head to keep the cold spring rain from going down his back, Chris ran to the building. He stood in the covered entryway shaking the water off then went inside.

Cigarette smoke billowed around him in a thick, stinky cloud as he searched for an empty table. Waving his hand in front of his face to clear the air, he spotted an empty stool at the bar. He sat down and tapped the polished but water-stained wooden countertop. "Scotch on the rocks," he told the bartender. His wife didn't need to know he broke his sobriety tonight. He needed a drink or two. Maybe more.

"Sure. Never seen you before. Are you new in town? Where'd you serve?"

"Just passing through. My flight was canceled. To answer your question, the U.S. Army, Korea, and Vietnam."

"Two-timer, huh?" The bartender set the drink on a paper napkin in front of him.

"Yeah." Chris sipped his drink. Not cheap scotch but not the expensive kind either. He glanced around the room. Through the swirling smoke, he spotted a pool table. Flags of the armed services hung from the ceiling. An American flag on a wooden pole stood in the corner.

Then he noticed the pictures on the wall. He figured they were deceased service members from the Garden City area. One photograph he recognized. Michael Roberts. The VFW honored him by adding him to the fallen.

"I'm Jeremy Harper, the Garden City VFW chapter commander. Welcome," the man on the stool next to him said.

Chris downed the rest of his glass. "Thanks. Another, please. Run me a tab," he told the bartender.

"Sure." The bartender refilled the glass. "Do you want something to eat?" He pointed at the menu written on the chalkboard. Fried bologna and grilled cheese sandwiches, chili, and fried chicken wings with Buffalo sauce, carrot sticks, and ranch dressing.

Yuk. Only if he wanted a case of salmonella or severe indigestion. "Nah." Chris should've taken Mrs. Roberts up on her dinner offer. The bar snacks of pretzels, peanuts, and potato chips would have to do.

"What's wrong?" Harper asked.

"Nothing," Chris replied.

"It's more than nothing, or you wouldn't be at a bar."

"I visited the family of someone who died in Cambodia."

"You serve with him?"

Chris shook his head. "No, only met him once."

Harper pointed at the pictures. "Who?"

"Michael Roberts." He downed the drink and ordered another. He'd sleep it off in his car tonight and shower at the truck stop. His flight wasn't until 0900 hours tomorrow morning. How many more times in his life would he fall off the wagon?

0730 Hours
April 12, 1976
Building 54 - Nathan Hale Hall
902nd Military Intelligence Group Headquarters
Ft. Meade, MD

Chris whistled from the parking lot to his office. Last Friday helped his conscience. The drinking, not so much. Drunk off his ass with Jeremy Harper buying him drink after drink, asking questions about Vietnam and his connection to Michael Roberts, he didn't remember anything after midnight. Who knows what he told him? His career and security clearance might be in jeopardy if the Army found out. The flight home seemed like forever with an upset stomach and a hangover headache the size of Texas.

But the alcohol did soften his soul in a scotch-flavored brine. His guilty conscience wouldn't let him stay quiet. When he told Kara what happened, he got off easy. Instead of a verbal flogging, he sat on the living room couch for a long one-sided calm lecture which he took with grace and no arguments. She was right. Alcohol was more of an enemy than the NVA or Viet Cong. It killed you slowly. Time to climb back on the wagon. At least until he fell off again. That was life. Stumble and keep picking yourself back up.

He regretted not visiting the Roberts after learning about their son's death. He'd always remember him as Mikey – a smiling kid who should be going to medical school, not buried in Kansas.

Tossing his keys on his desk, Chris turned to get his glass coffee pot to fill it in the break room and stopped. Sitting in a chair pushed into the far corner was an older, bald, overweight man wearing a wrinkled tan lightweight cotton suit. How did this guy gain access to his office inside a locked facility where it takes a high-security clearance to get past the guards at the front doors?

"How'd you get in here? Who in the hell are you?" Chris grabbed the coffee pot. It was his only weapon. His loaded Colt M1911A1 .45 caliber pistol was locked in his wall safe. Why maintain a way to defend himself? Sitting in the middle of an Army base with armed guards at the doors, this building was supposed to be secure. Someone screwed up.

The man raised both hands. "Easy, Colonel. I'm only here to talk."

Chris lowered the pot then placed it on the coil. "You didn't answer my question."

"My name is Stuart Cain. I'm the CIA attaché to the Army. I make sure all our combined operations run smoothly and by the numbers."

"Show me your credentials."

The man cackled like a sex-starved rooster. "I'm impressed. You're the first person other than the gate guards and the guy downstairs to ask me that in over a year." He pulled out a small, black case and flipped it out with a practiced flair.

Chris took the case then looked at the ID and gold Special Agent badge inside. They appeared legit. The laminated ID card had the name Stuart B. Cain beside the CIA Shield – a blue circle with a bald eagle head over a white shield. Inside the shield, a gold sixteen-point compass rose. His clearance level – Top-Secret.

Chris went to his desk, laid the case open on it, and dialed the switchboard.

"How can I help you?" the female operator asked.

"This is Colonel Patterson. Send two MPs to my office to pick up an intruder then connect me with CIA headquarters in Langley, Virginia." He was going to find out if this guy was for real. If not, arrest him for espionage against the United States. A charge punishable by death.

"Yes, sir," the operator said.

Chris listened to the phone ring a dozen times then it stopped. He heard clicks on the line as if he were being transferred to several locations. To where, he didn't know.

"Deputy Director Watts. Am I speaking with Colonel Patterson?" a low, growling male voice asked.

How'd he know? "Yes." *My encrypted phone number, stupid. I command an intelligence unit.*

"Is this call because of one of my agents, Stuart Cain?"

"Yes. I take it this is an official visit." *He's really CIA. Interesting.*

"It is. Anything else, Colonel Patterson?"

"No, sir." Chris hung up the phone. He went to his door and opened it. Two MPs were striding swiftly toward his office. "Go back to your posts," he ordered them.

"Are you sure, sir?" one of the men asked.

"Yes, I'm sure. Go! Now!"

The men saluted then headed to the elevator.

Chris shut the door and turned, crossing his arms. "Why are you here?" *I hate this melodramatic crap.*

"Interesting question. I'll ask the same one." Cain pointed at the 902nd MI Group crest on the wall. "Why are you here?"

"Orders."

"It's more than that, Patterson."

He knows. "Are you talking about my promotion and how it's tied into my connection to Colonel MacKenzie?"

"Bingo!"

Chris marched over to Cain, leaning over him. "This isn't a fucking game. What do you want?"

"I heard you visited Mr. and Mrs. Roberts. Did they tell you anything?" Cain asked.

Why's he interested in that? Did he follow me? I went there to pay my respects. Nothing more." *I'm not about to tell this asshole everything. I learned how he died and a brief description of their mission. He might blab to my CO and get me court-martialed for withholding information.*

"Because you met him in Vietnam and sent his nomination for the Army Commendation Medal?"

Shit! "Yes."

"I understand the soldier code. Never leave a man behind and all that honor stuff, Colonel. We have it in the CIA. Sometimes we have to leave a man behind to keep the country's secrets, and they become stars on a wall. Just make sure of where your loyalty lies."

Chris clenched his fists. "You can bet on that" *Duty to my country, loyalty to my friends. They aren't mutually exclusive.*

"As long as you understand your duties in the scheme of things, Colonel Patterson." Cain stood, brushed at the wrinkles in his pants, and left.

Ortiz ran into the office. "Who was that? He's not on the log."

Figures. "Don't ask." Chris handed Ortiz his empty coffee pot. "Go fill this, make me a double strong pot of coffee and hold my calls for the next hour…I have a few reports to finish." He didn't, he just needed time to think.

"Yes, sir." Ortiz left with the pot.

Chris sat at his desk. Lying on the blotter was a Marine KA-BAR and a note:

Be careful what you wish for. Don't cut your own throat. Loyalty has its limits.

Cain

He pulled the KA-BAR from the USMC/Eagle, Globe, and Anchor embossed brown leather sheath and checked the blade with his thumb. It was razor-sharp.

Ortiz returned and started the coffee. "Anything else, sir?"

"No. You have your orders." Chris waited until Ortiz left, resheathed the blade, and turned it over. On the back, stamped into the leather, J.J. MacKenzie – U.S. Army. This was Jackson's knife. Probably the one he carried on that mission. How did Cain get it? And what was that crack about cutting his own throat? He'd have to be careful from now on.

CHAPTER 25

1900 Hours
August 1, 1978
Delmonico's Restaurant
56 Beaver St
New York, NY 10004

"Table for two, sir? It'll be a long wait," said the maître d' in his black tuxedo and bow tie.

"You should have our reservation under Patterson." Chris straightened the tie of his black suit. He took two days of leave time for this special night. Kara looked beautiful in her long blue dress. They didn't drive for three hours, rent a hotel room, and get dressed up for nothing.

The maître d' ran his finger down the paper on his podium. "Patterson...Patterson," he mumbled. "Here it is. Table for two at seven o'clock." He grabbed two menus. "This way."

They followed him to a table toward the back of the elegant dining room. He seated them in the red-accented wooden chairs. Chris waited for Kara to sit first. The pictures he'd seen didn't do the place justice. Chandlers hung from the ceiling. Every table was covered with a fine white satin tablecloth. Filled water glasses were poised next to the china plates. Folded linen napkins and silverware sat next to the plates. A flickering candle in the center of the table completed the ambiance.

The maître d' handed them each a menu. "Enjoy. Your waiter will be with you shortly."

Even though he knew what he wanted, Chris looked at the menu – Prime Sirloin Steak, Filet Mignon, Veal Paillard, Lamb Chops, Veal Chop, Pork Chops, Half Chicken, Mixed Grill, Maine Lobster Tail, and Filet Mignon. The list of seafood and other dishes, while nice, didn't interest him.

"Honey, have you looked at these prices? Can we afford this?" Kara asked.

"Yes, I planned for it. I wanted our tenth anniversary to be special."

"Just the trip to New York was good enough for me."

"Not enough to give you this." Chris handed her a small black box.

Kara lifted the lid and held a pearl necklace up to her neck. "Chris, this is too much."

"Not for you, it isn't."

"I love you." Kara leaned over the table and kissed him.

The waiter approached the table. "Can I take your order?"

"Go ahead, Chris. I haven't decided yet."

"I'll take the Maine Lobster tail and Filet Mignon, medium, with Baked Alaska for dessert," Chris said.

"Good choice," the waiter said. "And you, ma'am?"

"The fettuccine with chicken, lobster, scallops, and mushrooms. I'll also have Baked Alaska. Bring us both a glass of Cabernet Sauvignon."

"I'll have the salads out to you shortly." The waiter gathered up the menus and left.

"Are you sure?" Chris made the drinking motion with his hand. "You know me and alcohol."

Kara smiled. "It's our anniversary. Promise me you'll be good."

"Promise." And he intended to keep it.

After dinner, dessert, and coffee, Chris heard a somewhat familiar female voice. He looked around to see if he was right. A few tables away sat a beautiful and curvy blond-haired woman in a black evening dress. Across the table from her was an older man wearing a dark blue double-breasted suit that cost more money than Chris made in a month.

"I'll be back in a few minutes." Chris didn't want Kara involved. She might rip the woman's heart out. He went to the table, stood behind the woman then cleared his throat. "Ahem."

She held out her wine glass without looking at him. "Get me another glass of Dom Perignon."

Chris crossed his arms and leaned back on his heels. "I'm not a waiter or a wine steward."

The woman turned in her chair. It was Carolyn, Jackson's ex-wife. Someone he didn't expect ever to meet again.

"Do I know you?" she asked.

Either she didn't remember him, which he found hard to believe since he was Jackson's best man in a full military wedding, or she was playing dumb for her husband, waiting for his next move. Chris didn't think she was that smart. More like a standard bubble-headed blond used as arm candy. "Yes."

128

Carolyn tapped her lips. "You do seem familiar and handsome in a rugged, outdoorsy sort of way. I love your brown eyes. Did we date once or twice?"

That made him mad. "No! Was it worth it?"

Her eyebrows went up. "Worth what?"

Chris held up the West Point class ring on his right hand. "Divorcing the finest man you'll ever meet."

"Now I remember you. You went to West Point with Jackson. You were his best man...Chris somebody."

"Patterson."

"To answer your question, yes, it was worth it. You make what...about two thousand dollars a month?"

"As a full Colonel in the Army, without combat pay, a little over that, but yes."

The man with her finally spoke. "I'm her husband, Gerald Moore. Would you care to explain what you want, Mr. Patterson?"

"I wanted to see what kind of slut your wife became, Mr. Moore. Jackson was too good for you, Carolyn."

Mr. Moore bowed up, sputtering at the insult. "He left her, refused to answer her letters and phone calls."

"Is that what she told you?" Chris asked.

"Yes."

"It's a bald-faced lie."

"How so?" Moore tapped the table. "She showed me the returned letters."

"Returned letters? I bet she faked them." Chris imitated holding a phone receiver to his ear. "You don't just call someone in Vietnam like they're across town. It takes a connection to a MARS station."

"I don't know what a MARS station is, but I can tell from your tone, it's difficult."

"Very. MARS means Military Auxiliary Radio System. It's a network of ham radio operators dedicated to helping soldiers call home."

"Okay, not that I care. So what. How'd she lie?"

"Jackson didn't abandon her or refuse to write to her. He was missing in action. A prisoner of war in North Vietnam for nearly a year. He pulled off the impossible by escaping and damn near died at the hospital."

Carolyn looked at Chris. He thought he saw a brief moment of concern on her face. No, he had to be imagining it. According to the records, she signed for the Western Union telegram. She already knew.

"Was he tortured?" Carolyn asked.

"Severely," Chris replied. "He damn near died because of the cruel and inhuman treatment."

"It doesn't matter. Didn't you know? He's a criminal now. AWOL. On the run from the Army."

"Oh, I know. I'm the man assigned to find him. Good day. Enjoy your miserable fucking life of money and not much else. It sure can't be…love." *Married to that ugly old-ass rich loser.* Chris returned to his table. "Let's go."

"Who was that?" Kara asked.

Chris smiled. "Jackson's ex. I went alone because I didn't want you to kill her."

0800 Hours
August 4, 1978
Building 54 - Nathan Hale Hall
902nd Military Intelligence Group Headquarters
Ft. Meade, MD

As Chris waited outside General Kinsey's office, he wondered why he'd been summoned. He researched each lead and turned in his reports. Right now, he had nothing to report.

The general's clerk exited from the inner office. "Go in, Colonel Patterson."

Chris marched in and stood at attention in front of the desk. "Colonel Patterson reporting as ordered, sir!"

General Kinsey stood. His eyes blazed as the veins in his forehead pulsed. "Why did you confront Gerald Moore on Tuesday? Did you know he's the CEO of a Forbes 500 company? The man's a millionaire with an apartment on 5th Avenue."

"No." *I guess they complained.*

"No, what, Colonel?"

"No, I didn't know he runs a Forbes 500 company. I never met or heard of him before Tuesday."

The general slammed his hands on the desk, leaning forward on them with his mouth screwed into a frown. "What is your malfunction, Patterson?"

"I didn't confront him, sir. I confronted his bitch of a wife."

"What! Why?" the general sputtered.

Chris smiled. He had the advantage of information. "Her name is Carolyn. She is Lieutenant Colonel MacKenzie's ex-wife. Mr. Moore didn't tell you that, did he? I happened upon her while taking my wife out for our tenth anniversary. It was a…happy accident, sir. I thought she might know something." A lie, but who cares. He was on a roll.

The general's attitude suddenly changed from anger to curiosity. "MacKenzie's ex, huh?"

"Yes, sir. She told me to fuck off, invoked her fifth amendment rights, and to go see her lawyer." Not really. The general doesn't need to know.

"Do you think she knows anything?"

"No, I checked her phone records a year ago. The only things in them were hairdressers, a few male escorts, taxis, and…a high-priced plastic surgeon." *From the looks of those saggy ass cheeks, he didn't do a good job.*

The general laughed. "Then you're the right person for the job. Sorry for the intrusion. Dismissed."

Chris saluted. "Yes, sir." He was getting good at lying to superior officers.

1200 Hours
August 22, 1978
Building 54 - Nathan Hale Hall
902nd Military Intelligence Group Headquarters
Ft. Meade, MD

Chris slammed the phone down on the cradle. "Ortiz, get in here!" he yelled.

Ortiz ran in, huffing. "What, sir?"

"Get me a plane on the tarmac at Tipton Army Airfield ASAP."

"Why, sir?"

"Got a tip that MacKenzie was spotted at Hyde Field four hours ago."

"That's less than five hundred miles away."

"Yeah, but the unmarked white Gulfstream II he arrived in took off ten minutes later."

"Headed where?"

131

"No idea. But we got word of an airliner hijacking. The plane landed at Provo, Utah. According to an FBI BOLO that just came over the wire, an unmarked white Gulfstream matching the description of the one at Hyde Field is stuck on the runway waiting for clearance to taxi."

"You think it's him, sir?"

"Maybe, but we won't know unless we get there. Given the FBI locked down the airport, that plane won't be leaving anytime soon. The feds go by their tried and true fucked up checklist on things like this. It should take hours or even days. Understood?"

Ortiz ran out of the office.

Chris opened his safe, grabbed his pistol, and relocked the safe. Now he had a chance to prove his worth.

1210 Hours
Ft. Meade, MD

As Ortiz drove the jeep along Mapes Road toward the base gate that would take them to Tipton Airfield, an OD green deuce and a half truck heading in the opposite direction swerved into their path.

"Look out!" Chris yelled.

They had two choices, a head-on collision with a nearly 13,000-pound truck or finding another path. Ortiz jerked the wheel to the right, running the jeep over the curb. The jeep bounced through the grass as Ortiz tried to brake and defensively steer around the obstacles in their path. With their speed and the ground wet and muddy, they skidded around as if on a patch of ice.

The stand of trees less than a hundred feet away got closer and closer.

Chris thought they could stop in time as the jeep slowed. But no such luck. He braced himself with his hands on the dashboard and feet pressed into the floorboard. The jeep struck the large trunk of an oak tree and stopped, flipping Chris over the raised windscreen onto the hood. He rolled off, striking the ground hard on his left shoulder, unable to breathe.

Several soldiers ran to their location. One helped Chris sit up as he held his ribs. His body felt pulled to a breaking point at both ends. Another soldier assisted Ortiz off the ground, sitting him beside Chris.

"What the fuck just happened?" Chris wheezed, trying to catch his breath.

Ortiz held a handkerchief to the bleeding cut on his head, probably from windshield glass. It broke on impact. The razor-sharp shards were scattered around the jeep. "I don't know, sir. That truck came into our lane."

"I know that. Why?"

"Broken tie rod, Colonel," the soldier beside Chris said.

Chris found that hard to believe. Their first big lead and a truck runs them off the road on the way to the airfield. Too convenient. Or the other option, just bad luck. He didn't believe in coincidences.

"An ambulance is on the way, sir," the same soldier said.

"Don't need it. Help me up." Chris held out his free hand. His other one gripped his left ribs. He glanced at the man's name tag. "Sergeant Rosenberg."

"Sir! You're hurt!"

"Wrong. I'm banged up a little." Chris didn't want to look like a wuss in front of these men. Leaders lead by example, not sitting on their asses. "Do I have to make it an order? Help me up." He shook his outstretched hand.

Rosenberg pulled Chris to his feet. He swayed a little then got his bearings.

"Sir. I think you need to go to the hospital."

"And I will but not in a meat wagon," Chris replied. "Do you have transportation?"

"A jeep, sir."

"Then help me to that jeep, Sergeant."

"Yes, sir." Rosenberg drew Chris' arm across his shoulders and took his weight.

As they walked past the deuce and a half parked on the shoulder, Chris bent enough to look under the truck. He didn't see a broken tie rod. That didn't mean there wasn't one. Only that he couldn't see it. Soldiers were clambering around and under the truck doing something.

0900 Hours
August 23, 1978
Married Officers Housing
Patterson Residence
Ft. Meade, MD

Kara helped Chris into his chair in the living room. She lifted his legs onto the hassock, turned on the television, kissed his forehead, and went to the kitchen. She allowed him to sleep instead of getting up at his usual time of 0500 hours to go for a five-mile run. Running wasn't in the cards for a few days.

He and Ortiz got lucky. They skated with minor injuries, treated at the hospital, and released. Right now, it didn't feel minor. He couldn't find a pain-free position. His ribs ached. While not broken, they were deeply bruised. It made breathing an excruciating experience. He didn't want the pain medication the emergency room doctor prescribed, preferring to take only aspirin. The narcotics made him see funny things that weren't there. For someone already disposed to having nightmares of wartime experiences, that was not a good thing. He didn't want to attack his wife in a drugged haze and hurt or possibly kill her thinking a gook was sneaking up on him.

Kara returned with a plate of scrambled eggs and a cup of hot coffee. She set the plate in his lap and the coffee on the table next to his chair. "Enjoy." She ran a tender hand down his cheek. Even that hurt.

"Thanks." Chris picked up his fork. He didn't feel like eating, but she fixed it for him, and he wouldn't disappoint her. This was the first time in their marriage she had the chance to nurse him back to health. He might as well enjoy it. The pain would go away soon. That's what the doctor said yesterday.

Kara returned to the kitchen.

Chris put a forkful of eggs into his mouth and chewed. Kara made him her special eggs with melted cheddar cheese. They tasted wonderful, bringing his stomach to life, telling him he was hungry.

A news blurb came on the TV about the airliner hijacking yesterday. He leaned closer to get a better look.

The camera panned across a Boeing 727. Men in black suits were dragging a man wearing jeans and a red shirt toward a waiting black van. Chris had to assume they were FBI agents and the hijacking suspect.

Close to the airliner sat a white Gulfstream II. Five men wearing black utility uniforms exited the plane carrying duffle bags and rifles. All Chris saw was their backs. While they looked like Jackson and the others from the rear, he couldn't be sure. The image wasn't clear enough. The men could be anyone. Since they were carrying gear, even FBI agents brought in for the rescue and the reason for the back shots was to protect their identity.

He hurt too much to get out of the chair to turn up the volume.

Kara came in. "Need anything?"

"Yeah, turn up the television."

"Sure. I saw this earlier." She turned the knob.

"Five CIA agents, here for refueling en route back to Langley, Virginia, helped rescue the 156 hostages onboard the airliner. Due to the volatile nature of the situation and their close proximity to the aircraft, the agents were given temporary authority to work within U.S. borders. No injuries were reported. Once the authorities check the airliner for any additional explosives, it will continue to its destination," the voice of the TV anchor said.

"Wow. Those people are really lucky those men were there," Kara said.

"Yeah," Chris replied. An overweight, balding man wearing a pink Hawaiian shirt and tan Bermuda shorts strolled into camera range. He recognized him immediately. Cain. *I guess those guys are CIA agents. Not Jackson and his men. It explains the unmarked plane. Wonder if it's the same one from Hyde Field?*

The phone rang on the end table. Kara picked it up. "Hello." She listened for a few seconds then hung up.

"Who was it?" Chris asked.

"He said his name is Stuart Cain. He's sorry about your accident. And something that doesn't make any sense."

"What?"

"Nice try."

Chris was confused. What did "nice try" mean?

CHAPTER 26

1100 Hours
August 1, 1980
Building 54 - Nathan Hale Hall
902nd Military Intelligence Group Headquarters
Ft. Meade, MD

Ortiz entered Chris' office, placed two envelopes in the inbox, and nodded, standing at a loose attention for further orders.

Chris returned the nod, picked up the top envelope, and looked at the return address. Department of the Army – Promotion Board – Washington, DC. He only had one person up for promotion and it took twice as long as usual. Probably because of the drawdown after the end of the Vietnam War and the kid was OCS. "Stand fast, Ortiz."

"Yes, sir." Ortiz put his hands behind his back.

Chris slit the envelope open and looked at the contents. He leaned back in his chair, tapping his finger on his lips. "Hmmm…congratulations, 1st Lieutenant Ortiz."

"Really, Colonel?" Excitement spread across the young man's face.

"Yes." Chris shook his head. Was he ever that young? He surely didn't act like Ortiz when his CO told him about his first promotion. Probably not. He'd already been to war. That day was so long ago.

Ortiz held his hand across the desk. "Thank you, sir."

Chris shook his hand then placed the announcement in it. "Take the rest of the day off and celebrate. Get your buddies to give you a good wetting down. Just remember, moderation. Be back here on Monday bushy-tailed and ready for new duties. Understood?"

"Yes, sir."

"Dismissed."

Ortiz bounced out of the room like an overinflated helium balloon.

Chris chuckled as he grabbed the other envelope. The name and address of the sender threw him for a loop. Colonel Norville Hammond – Norton Air Force Base, San Bernardino, California. The last he heard that asshole was in Fort Wainwright, Alaska.

He slit the envelope open with his pocket knife and pulled out the letter typed on plain white paper.

23 July 1980

Colonel Christopher Patterson
902nd Military Intelligence Group
Building 54 – Nathan Hale Hall
4554 Llewellyn Ave
Ft. Meade, MD 20755

Colonel Patterson,

While on a layover en route from a training conference to my command at Fort Wainwright, AK, I was eating dinner in the base mess hall with members of my staff. One of the Army officers assigned there for Blackhawk helicopter training bumped into me. I could have sworn that man was Lt. Colonel Jackson MacKenzie. He had graying hair but with the same height and build.

A member of his Blackhawk crew, Sergeant Valdez, said his name was Lt. Colonel Jackson Jones. That's quite a coincidence. That name sounds like an alias to me.

I asked around, only to find out all information on the Army personnel training here is classified. Some big upcoming operation for which I don't have clearance. I was told he's been at Norton for the past two months, and his service records are filed in the Army section at the headquarters building.

Could you look into this?

Colonel Norville Hammond
172nd Brigade Support Battalion
Ft. Wainwright, AK

Chris leaned back in his chair. Hammond thought Jackson was not only at Norton but openly training to fly Blackhawk helicopters. That idea was bizarre and ludicrous. How could Jackson fake all the records and official orders to pull that off? And why would he? The power of the United States Army was after him. Why would he trap himself on an Air Force base behind manned guard gates with no way out?

Hammond didn't say anything about Mason, Carter, or Blackwater. If Jackson were there, he wouldn't be there alone. Another nail in Hammond's crazy idea. The man must be losing his mind in the freezing cold and Alaskan snowbanks. But Chris needed to check the lead. You never know.

Chris found the phone number in his Rolodex and called the records division at Norton AFB.

"Norton Air Force Base Records section, Senior Airman Barnes speaking," said the man who picked up the line.

"This is Colonel Decker, U.S. Army. I'm the commanding officer of the 902nd MI. Do you have access to the service jackets of Army personnel assigned for training at Norton?"

"Yes, sir. Who are you looking for?"

"Lieutenant Colonel Jackson Jones. He's training on Blackhawks."

"That name sounds familiar. I'll be back in a few minutes."

Click. Easy listening music echoed from the earpiece as the airman put him on hold.

Chris drummed his fingers on the desk as he waited. He hated this music. Rock and roll was more his style.

It seemed like forever before Barnes returned to the line.

"Colonel Decker, are you still there?" Barnes asked.

"Yes. What did you find out?" Chris put his feet on his desk. He might as well get comfortable.

"I'll tell you what I can, sir. Lieutenant Colonel Jones is being certified on Blackhawks. He's been here for two months. Since he's training for a top-secret operation, I can't give you any more information."

"I have a top-secret clearance, son. I'm head of an intelligence unit."

"Yes, sir. I confirmed that while you were on hold. But this is compartmentalized need to know," Barnes replied.

Interesting. "And I don't need to know. Who has access?"

"The President, Joint Chiefs, the CIA director, and those involved in the operation."

"Short list. Can you tell me about his record?"

"Very little. Graduated from OCS. Huey pilot. Served in three tours in Vietnam with the 101st Airborne. DSC, Silver Star, DFC, Bronze Star, Air Medal, and three Purple Hearts."

"What's his birthday?"

"May 29th, 1935."

Around the same age as me, but I've never heard of him. "Anything else? Can you tell me his social security number or his last posting?"

"Sorry, sir, but no. I'm pushing my orders on these records telling you as much as I did. This operation is very hush-hush if you get my meaning."

"Understood. Let me ask you this. Do those records look like forgeries to you?"

"No, sir. They are official Army documents with all the correct signatures and watermarks. I've seen enough of these to know."

"Thanks, Airman." Chris hung up the phone. That was a colossal waste of his time. He should have known coming from an idiot like Hammond.

1400 Hours
August 1, 1980
Building 54 - Nathan Hale Hall
902nd Military Intelligence Group Headquarters
Ft. Meade, MD

General Manzarek stormed into Chris' office. "Where's your aide? His desk is unmanned."

Chris stood from his chair, cringing on the inside. The general was mad. "I gave him the day off. His promotion came down the pike today, sir." He didn't like his new commanding officer. General Manzarek, being small in stature at five-six, had a giant chip on his shoulder with anyone taller than him. Which was almost everyone. He was superior in rank only. The man had a reputation in Vietnam for getting men killed on under-planned, useless operations. His casualty rate was over fifty percent.

Manzarek cocked his head. "Okay. You should've had someone man his desk and take care of his duties, Colonel."

"Yes, sir." Chris accepted the dressing down. That was the procedure, but he didn't feel the need. It was Friday.

"Did you get one of these from Colonel Hammond?" Manzarek handed Chris a piece of paper.

A quick look confirmed it was an almost exact copy of the one he received this morning. "Yes, sir," Chris replied.

"Did you check on his accusations?"

Chris pointed at the chair in front of his desk. "Please sit, General. Yes, I did."

Manzarek sat in the chair. "And?"

Chris returned to his chair. "I spoke with Senior Airman Barnes in the records section at Norton. He confirmed Lieutenant Colonel Jones is training on Blackhawks and has been there for two months."

"What else? I know you didn't leave it at only that."

"No, sir. He confirmed all the records are official documents. Jones' file is currently compartmentalized as need to know as he's training for an upcoming top-secret operation. The only people with access are the President, Joint Chiefs, CIA director, and those involved."

"Thanks for following up, Patterson. I thought it was really far out there to believe an Army fugitive was openly training on an Air Force base on Army Blackhawks. Hammond must be imagining things."

Chris smiled. "My thoughts exactly, sir." Not that it couldn't happen. Jackson was gung ho enough to try it. And from the report about Cambodia, he has worked for the U.S. government in the past. With the CIA involved, those records could be undetectable forgeries with confirmable backstories. But Chris didn't care. He did his duty, and the general was satisfied. Why push his luck.

1600 Hours
January 5, 1981
Anderson, GA

Chris slammed the passenger door shut. He didn't wait for Ortiz and walked with a purpose instead of running to the jail in Anderson, Georgia. The county lockup was an indistinct concrete cinder block building in a small town with a population of less than a thousand people.

According to the dispatch from the sheriff, Jackson and Lt. Carter were caught fueling their truck at a gas station, and they gave up. Handing over their weapons without a fight. That didn't sound like Jackson or Carter. What was going on?

The even better question, now what was Chris going to do? He had to follow his orders and take the two men into custody. How would Jackson react to being handcuffed? Would he fight or go quietly?

Chris entered the jail and approached the manned counter in the lobby. "I'm Colonel Patterson." He glanced over as Ortiz joined him from the parking lot. "You should be expecting us."

The deputy nodded. "Yes, sir. We are. That didn't take long," the man said in a slow, southern drawl. He looked at his watch. "We only sent that teletype out six hours ago."

"That's what happens when you have priority. Can I see the prisoners?"

"Sure. Is it just the two of you?"

"No! I've got a squad of MPs from Fort Benning waiting outside with a secure transport van."

"Okay, just making sure. You need to hand over your weapon, Colonel, Lieutenant. Only deputies are allowed to carry in the jail area."

Not a good idea. Jackson and Carter could take them in a heartbeat. Nothing about this made sense. "Understood." Chris removed his Army-issue Colt M1911A1 .45 caliber pistol from his holster as Ortiz did the same. They unloaded the pistols and slid them across the counter to the deputy.

"Sign here." The deputy turned around a green-bound logbook. "You'll get them back when you leave." He placed the two pistols in a lockbox behind him.

Chris then Ortiz signed next to the serial number of their pistol.

"Now, take us to see them," Chris ordered.

"Yes, sir." He picked up the phone handset. "I've got two Army guys here to pick up the prisoners." He listened for a moment then hung up. "The sheriff will be here in a moment."

"Copy that." Chris picked up a magazine from the counter, *Law Enforcement Weekly*. He thumbed through the pages looking for anything interesting and found nothing.

A portly man wearing a khaki shirt with a five-pointed gold star on the left side entered the lobby from the door leading to the back of the station. His belly overlapped his gun belt, and the blue Smith & Wesson .357 revolver flopped around in an unsecured holster. If he was an example of the deputies in this town, why did Jackson and Carter give up? With their Special Forces training, they could take them without breaking a sweat.

"I'm Sheriff Bean. Come with me to see the prisoners." The man swiped his keycard in the reader, held the door open, and followed them inside.

Chris and Lt. Ortiz waited for the man in the narrow hallway. They had to flatten themselves against the wall and suck in deeply for the sheriff to get around them. It was a good thing they were in excellent physical shape, or they'd have been smashed flat.

Sheriff Bean shuffled along like he didn't have a care in the world until he arrived at another hallway and turned left. He opened the door with his keycard and stepped aside. "Go on in," the sheriff said.

"Thank you." Chris straightened his OD-green cotton fatigue shirt and went inside, flanked by Ortiz. The room contained three dingy six-by-eight barred cells that looked straight out of an old gangster movie. A green wool blanket-covered cot was at one end with a single overhead bare bulb, a toilet, and a sink. Each cell had a barred window near the low seven-foot ceiling.

Chris saw a man in the center cell and another in the one at the end. Both men stood from their bunks. That's when Chris' internal alarm bells started ringing. Even in the grayness of the room, the taller of the two men didn't look tall. He was about five foot ten at the most and overweight, but not to the extent of the sheriff. The other man was even shorter. Jackson was six foot one, and Carter was five foot ten. Who were these men? But he had to make sure.

Squaring his shoulders, Chris marched over to stand at the junction of the two cells. "I'm Colonel Patterson. Identify yourselves!"

The man at the end turned. His craggy, pockmarked face sneered at Chris with yellowed, rotten teeth. "Why do I care who you are, Army boy?"

Boy? Chris clenched his fists. This man sure wasn't Jackson. The man in the center cell turned to face Chris. A deep scar ran across his cheek. He gave Chris the same nasty sneer.

"What's it to you, doughboy?" the man said.

Chris shook his head, nodded to Ortiz, and exited the cellblock. He stopped to face the sheriff. "Who are those men?"

"MacKenzie and Carter," the sheriff replied. "That's why we contacted you."

"Did they tell you that?"

"No, I recognized them from the APBs."

"Recognized? They don't look like them or match their descriptions in any way, shape, or form. Didn't you send their prints to the FBI to make sure?"

"No. I didn't feel the need. That costs us money," the sheriff said.

"Then maybe you should spend some. Those men are not Carter and MacKenzie. I don't know who they are. If you don't want a lawsuit for false arrest, I suggest you figure out their names and find out if they are wanted." Chris pointed at the door. "What names did they give you?"

"Brody Gideon and Brent Colton."

"I would run those names and fingerprints through NCIC. You'll probably get a hit. Come on, Ortiz. We're leaving. This was a giant waste of our time." *Stupid hick town sheriff.* Chris stomped out to the lobby with Ortiz trying to keep up to retrieve his weapon. Now he had to do paperwork informing the general of the mistake and their expenses. He was sure to get a stiff one-sided lecture over this foul-up. One that wasn't within his control. An occurrence happening all too frequently with false leads coming in from citizens and law enforcement looking for a big score.

What he really hated. This wild goose chase interrupted his wife's birthday. He'd get her a dozen roses and a box of her favorite chocolate candies before going home. At least he could give her good news. It wasn't Jackson.

CHAPTER 27

1900 Hours
October 25, 1983
Married Officers Housing
Ft. Meade, MD

As Chris taped a cardboard pumpkin decoration to the outside of his front door, the phone inside the house rang. He jumped off the stepstool and ran inside to the kitchen, catching the phone on the fifth ring.

"Colonel Patterson speaking," he said, balancing the phone on his shoulder as he placed the masking tape back into the junk drawer.

"Colonel, it's Lieutenant Ortiz. We just got a sighting report over the wire about Lieutenant Colonel MacKenzie."

"Where?" Chris pulled the phone cord long enough and sat at the kitchen table with a pad of paper and a pen.

"That's what is confusing, sir. Grenada."

"Grenada!" He knew about the coup led by the Grenadian military nine days ago. His security clearance afforded him the knowledge of the U.S.-led invasion – Operation Urgent Fury – that kicked off early this morning. What he didn't know was Jackson's role. Was he working for the Marxists - the People's Revolutionary Army? Or had the U.S. government hired him again like Cambodia or another rumor – the failed hostage rescue in Iran. He quickly threw out the Marxist idea. Jackson would never be a mercenary for hire - one of the Army's vicious lies about him. This was his first real lead since he took this assignment. The others were all dead ends. The brass was starting to wonder about his sincerity and convictions.

"Colonel, did you hear me?" Ortiz said.

"No, sorry. Static on this end. What?" Chris asked.

"The information, while not confirmed, says MacKenzie was injured somehow and currently in surgery aboard the U.S.S. *Independence*."

"Try to get confirmation on that. Anything about the others?"

"Yes, sir. According to the descriptions, Lieutenant Carter and Sergeant Blackwater are with him along with another man."

"Captain Mason?"

"No, sir. At six to six foot one, too tall for him. And we heard that rumor Captain Mason died of cancer earlier this year."

I forgot about that. "Okay, what about Harry Russell?"

"I don't think so, sir. No limp. Nothing about the subject missing a left foot. If anything, it says the exact opposite. The man took an active part in a firefight with Grenadian forces."

"A firefight. Why didn't you say that before?" *That tells me a lot. I wonder who's helping him?*

"That's where it came up in the communique, sir."

"Understood. Get us and an armed squad on an immediate flight to Barbados. And contact the U.S.S. *Independence* once they're off radio silence and ask the Captain about MacKenzie and the others."

"Already got a C-130 diverted to the airfield for a priority flight, and 1st Squad is ready to depart."

"Excellent." Chris checked his wristwatch. 1905 hours. "I'll get dressed and be there in thirty minutes. Great job, Captain. If we catch MacKenzie, there may be an accommodation in it for you."

"Thank you, sir."

Chris hung up. He looked over at Kara staring at him from the kitchen doorway.

"Did I hear right? You found Jackson in…Grenada? Isn't that in the Caribbean? And we just invaded Grenada, according to the radio." Kara asked.

They already announced it. "Yes, the Caribbean. Just a rumor he's…" He wondered about telling her the facts. "He's been injured and is on one of our carriers."

"I heard. The *Independence.* What are you going to do?"

"I won't know until I get there." Chris grabbed her in his arms. "Depends on him. Don't worry. I haven't forgotten my promise. I won't box him in, but I won't shirk my duty either."

"Good. That's all I ask. I don't want to lose either of you. I've already lost too much."

She's talking about Amanda. Chris kissed her and ran upstairs to get dressed in his newly-issued camouflage BDUs where he grabbed his go-bag from the bedroom closet. He had less than twenty minutes to get to Tipton Army Airfield. It wouldn't do for him, as the unit commanding officer, to be the last one to board the plane.

CHAPTER 28

1200 Hours
October 31, 1983
Grantley Adams International Airport
Seawell, Christ Church
Barbados

Chris paced back and forth next to the fence near the security gate leading onto the parking area north of Runway 27. They'd been waiting in the hotel for the last five days without a lead. He'd watched the president's address about the invasion of Grenada on a nineteen-inch television in his room.

This morning an NIS agent onboard the carrier U.S.S *Independence* relayed an encrypted communication to the 902nd Military Intelligence Group that a plane carrying Jackson and his men would arrive soon.

Near his location sat an all-white unmarked Grumman Gulfstream II being refueled and prepared by a ground crew for takeoff. A man wearing a military-type black-brimmed blue cover and dressed in a white shirt and black pants sat on the boarding stairs.

A Navy C-2 Greyhound with U.S.S *Independence* tail markings approached the airport from the east. It made a bouncy landing on Runway 27 and taxied to an area one hundred feet from the security gate.

His squad of five men, dressed in camouflage BDUs, black MP helmets, and armbands, unslung their M16s and pointed them at the airplane as the ground crew chalked the tires.

"What do you, for fuck's sake, think you're doing?" Chris ran down the line, slapping the muzzles toward the ground. "Are you going to open fire on a bunch of civilians or the Navy?" He went to the center of the line. "This is a foreign country. Do you want to start an international incident?"

"But, sir," Sergeant Early, the most senior man in the squad at twenty-one years old, said at the end of the line, slinging his rifle. "What if they fire on us?"

Chris got into his face. "With what? We haven't seen anyone yet." He went over to the security forces at the gate. "Why was our flight line status revoked?"

"I don't know," the main guard said. "It came from above." He pointed at the half-dozen Barbados airport security officers guarding the entrance/exit gate. "Don't do something stupid."

"We won't. Above?" Chris ground his teeth together. "Who?" *Sounds like someone with power.*

The guard shrugged. "Just following orders."

"Colonel, someone's coming," Early cried out.

Chris ran to the fence. A man wearing new-looking Marine Corps marked camouflage BDUs, black jump boots, and a black U.S.S *Independence* CV-62 ball cap walked down the ramp with a green standard-issue Army duffle bag on his shoulder. The bag blocked any view of his face. He climbed the stairs of the Gulfstream and disappeared inside.

Behind him came two similarly dressed men carrying duffle bags on their shoulders and slung M16s, Carter and Blackwater.

"Sir," Early yelled, unslinging his M16. "They have rifles."

"Put that weapon back on your shoulder, Sergeant, unless you want to be a private in the next few minutes," Chris ordered. "They're slung like yours should be." *He gets transferred when we get home. Too much of a hothead.* He returned to the guard gate. "We have a job to do. Let us on airport property!"

"No," the guard replied, locking the gate with an industrial-sized padlock then unslinging and charging his rifle.

As Carter and Blackwater ferried gear to the Gulfstream, Jackson, dressed like the others, with his left arm in a black nylon immobilization sling, descended the ramp. He walked up to the fence, looking pale as a ghost in the early afternoon sunlight and holding his bad arm tight to his body.

"They're not letting you come over here, are they, Chris?" Jackson said, his tone subdued, pain-filled, and hoarse.

Chris met him on the other side. "No. Security revoked our flight line clearance when the Navy plane landed. Did you have something to do with that, MacKenzie?" *He looks terrible. The rumor about him being wounded is true. Pretty bad from his appearance.*

"Didn't know you were here. How would I do that? I've been flat on my back with a chest tube in my side for five days. I'd invite you over, but someone with more power said *no*. Have a nice flight home. I'm hoping for a smooth one to stay off the pain meds."

Geez, that's not good. "That plane's unmarked. Whose is it?"

Jackson snickered. "No idea. Never asked. My guess, C-I-A. The fact it's unmarked should tell you something." He grunted as he stepped on a large rock then doubled over and vomited all over the ground. Chunky liquid splashed around his boots.

He looks like shit. Chris crossed his arms, concerned that Jackson was about to collapse into a lifeless heap and he had no way to get to him. "How bad were you hit?"

Jackson spat on the ground. He slumped against the fence as his legs shook like leaves in a stiff wind. "The round collapsed my lung and broke my shoulder blade. It's taking all of my control to stand here and talk to you. I'm not the one giving the orders. Someone else is pulling the strings. Head home. They're not going to let you over here until we leave."

Already figured that out. "Just between us. What's going on? How many of these missions have you taken for whoever owns that plane?" *Looks like the one from Provo.*

"The number, no idea—too many. We've been in over a dozen different countries doing hostage rescue, intelligence, and dignitary protection. That's not counting the ones for the FBI, ATF, NSA. The list of acronyms is too large to count. The Army wants to throw us in a hole. Everyone else wants us to work for them in the name of national security. I wish someone would make up their mind. All we want is our lives back."

That's a lot. Someone is working them to death. "Why work for the government with warrants over your heads? For money?" Chris eyed Jackson one more time, wondering how he'd answer that last question. *Let's see what he does.*

Jackson gripped the chain link fence so hard his knuckles turned white. That apparently pissed him off. "No! All we have asked for is the evidence to clear our names. Tell your CO that! I don't care anymore! All I want is to go home and live my life in peace. We're tired of being used and abused, then getting nothing except empty promises." He sucked in a deep breath and sagged nearly to his knees before straightening.

"Are you going to turn them down the next time they ask?" Chris hoped Jackson would say *no.* This situation would get him killed one day. If he was innocent and it looked more like that every day, that would be a crying shame.

"That won't happen until my shoulder heals." Jackson glanced over his good shoulder.

Blackwater was waving at him from the Gulfstream stairs.

"I have to go. By the way, I'm a full Colonel. I made the promotion list in 1972. Look it up. Someone told me it's easy to find. Et tu, Brute, Chris?" Jackson turned and headed toward the Gulfstream.

Et tu, Brute? He just compared me to Brutus. I didn't betray him. Who did? Chris watched him walk. Jackson's gait wasn't steady. He stumbled a couple of times and nearly face-planted himself into the hot asphalt. That had Chris concerned.

At the top of the aircraft stairs, Jackson turned to face him with the hint of a smile on his face.

Patterson placed two fingers against his hat brim as a small gesture of their former friendship. One he hoped to fix in the future. He let him have his way out by not forcing the issue with the airport security guards or the airport management.

Jackson copied him, and stepped into the plane, swallowed up by the shadows.

The cabin door closed. Within minutes, the Gulfstream took off into the clear blue sky. Chris couldn't use the transponder to track the plane without a tail number. Something told him even if he could, it wouldn't matter anyway. The plane was unregistered. Maybe the CIA was involved. What in the hell was going on?

CHAPTER 29

1100 Hours
November 5, 1983
Russell Residence
San Clemente, CA

Chris parked his rental car at the curb in front of a white house with red brick trim. Two vehicles sat in the driveway – a 1966 immaculate blue Pontiac GTO two-door hardtop and an ancient dirt brown rusted Ford Bronco that had seen better days.

The front porch had colorful flowers in the stone-walled flower beds. In the center of the yard, a twenty-foot flag pole with a gold ball on top held an American flag that flapped in the breeze. He walked up the driveway, came to attention, and saluted the flag.

He knocked on the door, not sure what to expect. Would Harry tell him to stick it and slam the door in his face?

Straightaway, he heard a dog barking inside the house getting closer then scratching. *Does he have a guard dog? I might after Hammond's personal threats. Or I'd just shoot the bastard with an incendiary round. Leave no ballistic evidence while he cooks from the inside.*

The door swung open. Harry stood there holding a large black Labrador retriever by the collar. The dog jumped at him. Chris stepped back.

"Don't worry. He won't bite you," Harry said, holding the collar tightly.

"That's what everyone says until someone gets bit," Chris replied, eyeing the large white teeth in the dog's drooling mouth.

Harry laughed. "Yeah, they do. Stay right where you are. Don't come in. Come on Bo." He led the dog away, leaving the front door wide open.

Chris knew this was a test to see what he'd do. That was Harry's style. Hammond would have walked on in.

Harry returned to the door. "Isn't the cease and desist order still valid?"

"It is, but I'm here unofficially." Chris pointed at his civilian clothes, jeans, a gray polo shirt, and hiking boots.

"Unofficial, huh? Why?" Harry's tone sounded as if he didn't believe him.

Chris could feel skepticism rolling off Harry in tsunami-sized waves. "Because I want to know what happened, damn it!"

Harry scrutinized him for a moment. "Come on in. But if I ever feel this is an official business visit, I will file a complaint with the courts."

"Duly noted." Chris stepped across the threshold and looked around. While it was a standard layout with three bedrooms, a living room, kitchen, and two bathrooms, the house was decorated nicely. Framed original prints and pictures were hung on the white painted walls. One caught his eye, Jackson in his class A uniform wearing a Green Beret and captain's bars. He knew that picture. Graduation from Special Forces training with Harry.

The spacious living room off to the left of the entry hall held a brown sofa, loveseat, two leather recliners, a console television, and a stereo.

Harry pointed at the recliners. "Have a seat."

Chris sat in the closest recliner while Harry sat in the other.

A tall, beautiful woman with delicate features, long brown hair and wearing a lavender pantsuit, entered from the kitchen door with a notepad and pen. "Hello. Harry told me you're Colonel Patterson."

Harry knows how to pick them. "Chris, please. I'm not here in any official capacity, Mrs. Russell. I know you work for a newspaper. I'm not a Hammond clone. That guy is a bastard."

Harry and his wife glanced at each other in surprise.

"Chris." She smiled at him. "I'm Gabby."

Chris smiled. "Nice to meet you." He had to garner their confidence. Hammond tried several illegal activities involving the Russells – wiretapping their phones, breaking into their house, and surveillance.

Gabby pulled a chair from the corner of the room and sat with them, scribbling on her notepad.

A young boy about ten years old in a baseball uniform and tall for his age ran into the living room. "Dad, I'm headed over to Teddy's."

Harry pointed at the boy. "Chris, meet my son...Jackson Joseph Russell."

He did that to be dramatic. Chris held out his hand. "Bet they call you JJ."

The boy's eyes lit up as he shook Chris' hand. "Yeah, after my uncle. Do you know him? Were you in the Army with him?"

"JJ," Harry cautioned with a low growl in his voice.

The kid shrugged, throwing up his hands. "What, Dad?"

Chris wanted to knock some sense into Harry. "Yes. I was his West Point roommate."

"So you're the guy trying to catch him."

They must tell him everything about what's going on with Jackson. "Yes…but that's not why I'm here."

"Go on over to Teddy's," Harry butted in. "Be home at 1600 to clean up. Dinner's at 1700."

"Yes, Dad." JJ grabbed a baseball bat and glove from the end table then exited the house.

"I wasn't going to bug him about Jackson," Chris said.

"It's not that. They're due at baseball practice in thirty minutes. Teddy's dad is taking them."

"Oh." Something he didn't understand. Parenthood. If his daughter had lived, they'd be only three years apart. He cringed. If JJ had known Amanda, they could have dated or become friends like Kara and Jackson. That felt weird.

Then Harry shocked him. "I heard you lost your daughter."

"I did. Stillborn. The cord prolapsed around her throat. We named her Amanda Elizabeth."

Gabby placed her hand over her mouth. "I'm so sorry."

"It's okay." Chris tried hard to keep the emotion out of his voice. "It was years ago."

"Why didn't you adopt?" Gabby asked.

"DHS took a dislike to my Vietnam service and the orphanage, even though the Army cleared me. We bucked it through the courts and lost. They make the rules."

"I know. That really sucks. Okay, Chris. Out with it," Harry said.

"First, I'm sorry I haven't visited you before this. How's your foot?"

"Which one? The good one." Harry pulled up his left pant leg, reviling his prosthetic. "Or the fake one."

Chris resisted the urge to roll his eyes. "The fake one. No limp."

"Worked hard at the VA to get rid of it."

"That's another thing. How'd you wind up there before completely healing? That's not—"

"Procedure." Harry completed the sentence. "I tried to find out what happened to JJ. I kept running into brick wall after brick wall. It took blackmailing General Paymore to get into Bragg to see him."

"His little midnight liaison with the hooker at the ABC bar?"

Harry grinned like a toothy wolf. "Yes."

"Excellent." Chris took a deep breath. "About that mission?"

"The art museum?"

"Yeah."

"I wasn't there. But I did help plan it."

"You saw the orders?" *I know Harry. He's an honest man. No way would he make that up.*

"Yes. Is that why you're here? Having second thoughts about your assignment?"

Chris nodded. "Yes. Too many things don't add up."

"Because you know him so well?"

"You just hit the nail on the head, Harry. But as you've found out, being upfront about trying to figure this out is a career killer. I'd already been passed over for promotion twice because someone high up caught me snooping, and I didn't know it."

"And the Army brass was going to retire you and offered you the promotion to locate JJ?"

"Uh-huh. They used it as leverage for me to accept the posting. I figured it would be easier to work from the inside than out. Did you know my wife and JJ were friends growing up at Pendleton? Her father is one of the men his father saved at the Battle of Okinawa and got nominated for the Medal of Honor."

Harry looked over at Gabby then back at Chris. "No! I knew he introduced you to Kara, but I didn't know that. Bet you're getting an earful at home about this."

"This is great stuff." Gabby turned the page on her notebook and kept writing.

Just like a reporter. "Yes, the assignment put a small rift in our relationship," Chris said. "I promised Kara I wouldn't box Jackson in and force a confrontation. I could've at Barbados and didn't." *See if that gets a reaction.*

"Wouldn't know. I wasn't there," Harry said stone-faced.

I understand why he's lying to me. I would, too, after taking Hammond's huge load of bullshit. "If you say so." *Would he lie to protect JJ? Probably, but why would the Army go after everyone if the orders aren't real? That means they are.*

"He was here the entire time," Gabby said. "We watched the President's address together."

They don't trust me. Understandable. "Got it."

"But I heard through the grapevine...JJ is healing well," Harry said, patting his left shoulder.

Chris sighed in relief. Harry took pity on him. He needed to know that piece of info. Jackson looked horrible when he climbed on the plane. "Thanks."

"What are you going to do?" Harry asked.

"Stay, or would you rather have someone like that crazy bastard Hammond who isn't sympathetic to JJ?"

"Oh, hell no!" Harry exclaimed.

Chris leaned forward on his elbows. He needed to find out. "Do you know about the fight JJ and I had at Gunslinger's?"

"Of course." Harry looked at his hands. "You were both drunk."

"Yeah. Why did JJ get drunk that night? He normally doesn't drink."

"Ahhh…" Harry glanced over at his wife as if unsure what to say.

"Come on, Harry. You know why. JJ confides in you."

Harry sighed. "General Thomas ordered him to get a physical to return to full duty. The doctor chewed him out about his weight. JJ thought everyone was ganging up to force him into retirement. He was having a hard time dealing with the POW camp. And he heard the rumor you killed those kids on purpose. It felt like a punch in the gut. Another My Lai. He found out the truth later and regretted what happened. He still kicks himself about it."

"Thanks, Harry." Now he knew what started the fight. Alcohol, stupidity, and scuttlebutt. "Then, I'll take my leave of you." Chris started to stand, but Harry stopped him with a hand on his arm.

"The next time I hear from JJ, do you want me to tell him any of this?" Harry asked. "I know he wants to apologize to you."

Chris shook his head. "No. Please keep it between us. I want to tell him." *I need to.*

Harry let go of his arm. "That's a dangerous cat and mouse game you're playing with the Army. It could get you burned."

"I know."

"What if CID finds out?"

"I'll deal with it." Chris stood. "I'm willing to take that chance just like you." He got what he wanted. Now, what did he do with it?

CHAPTER 30

```
1000 Hours
November 7, 1983
Married Officers Housing
Ft. Meade, MD
```

Kara met Chris in the entry hall as he laid his garment bag over his small suitcase.

"Was it worth paying out of our savings for that plane ticket?" Kara asked.

"I think so," Chris replied, pointing at the living room. He followed Kara to the couch and sat beside her. "You wanted me to find out what's going on."

"Well?" Kara crossed her arms.

"I'm sure Harry Russell knows where Jackson is staying."

"Honey?"

"I didn't push him about it. To tell you the truth, I didn't want to know. It ties my hands. But I did meet Harry's son." Now for the surprise. "Jackson Joseph Russell."

"They named him after Jackson?" Kara squealed. "How old is he? What's he like?"

"He's ten and all boy. Tall with brown hair like his dad. Plays baseball. And he's protective of his Uncle Jackson."

"Uncle Jackson? Terrific. I'd love to meet him one of these days."

"I'll try to make that happen. I did find out one thing."

"What's that?"

"Harry helped plan the art museum mission and saw the orders. I believe him. Losing his foot did him a favor."

"I wouldn't exactly call that a favor. But go on," Kara said.

Chris looked at his feet. No, he'd rather have his foot. Harry probably would too. Being an amputee and Vietnam veteran closed a lot of doors. "Jackson's okay. Harry denies being there. But I expected that. What else could he say and not get fingered for harboring a fugitive."

"What are you going to do?"

Chris laughed. "Harry asked the same question. I'm going to carry on like this trip didn't happen. If I see JJ again, I'll try to convince him to turn himself in and let the system work."

"That didn't work out well for him the last time from the rumors you've heard."

"No. He got big-time shafted. Regulations weren't followed or outright ignored. The same thing happened to Harry. This time JJ has an ace in the hole. Me. I'll do everything I can to make sure that crap doesn't happen again."

"At least until they arrest you or force you into retirement."

"There's always that. I don't think arresting me is an option. It would cause too many questions, and a court-martial would only exacerbate them tenfold. Whoever is behind this wouldn't want that to happen. Retirement gives me the right to work in the open."

"There's a third option. They could kill you," Kara suggested.

Chris grabbed her in a hug. *I'll keep a pistol hidden in the living room from now on. With the CIA possibly involved, I don't want to disappear suddenly.* "Let them try. The body bags going into the meat wagon won't be mine. But now I know for certain something is going on behind the veil of *classified*."

Kara nodded. "Since you're still on leave, what are your plans?"

Chris knew what she wanted from the look in her eyes. It had been a long time since they'd been intimate with each other. Work took the fun out of home life. He brushed the hair out of her eyes. "How about we go mess up the bed?"

"I love that idea." Kara ran a finger down his chest to his crotch. She popped open the top button of his blue jeans.

Just that action brought on an erection as his pants tightened. He scooped her up and carried her to the bedroom. Who cared about the Army? His wife was all that mattered.

0900 Hours
December 1, 1983
Building 54 – Nathan Hale Hall
902nd Military Intelligence Group Headquarters
Ft. Meade, MD

Chris stopped at Ortiz's desk on the way to his office. "Do you have anything for me?" He took a bite of his glazed donut he snagged from the break room. They were fresh today, not stale, rock-hard leftovers from the night shift. Only edible dunked in coffee.

A smile spread across Ortiz's face. He looked like he'd won the Super Bowl betting pool. "Yes, sir. I spoke with a Doctor...ahhh." He pulled a piece of paper from a pile on his desk. "Colburn at Steele Memorial Hospital in Salmon, Idaho."

"And?" Chris bit off another chunk of his donut.

"He faxed me this." Ortiz handed Chris a copy of a death certificate dated May 3, 1983. On the name line was William Lewis Mason Jr. Cause of death: Pneumonia. Contributing factors: Respiratory arrest due to Pulmonary edema and Stage IV bone cancer.

Chris handed the copy back to Ortiz. "What else did he say?"

Ortiz looked at his notes. "Two men brought Mason to the emergency room on April 9th of this year with a broken leg. X-rays confirmed the leg was shattered. Dr. Colburn thought it seemed strange for the leg to shatter simply by stepping in a hole. He ran some tests and determined Mason had bone cancer, and it had spread to his organs."

"What a terrible way to go for a soldier. Lying in a fucking hospital bed," Chris spat. He wondered what caused the cancer. Was it that crap in the orange-striped barrels they sprayed all over Vietnam? Should he worry? He got soaked in it a couple of times.

"Yes, sir. I agree. I faxed him pictures of MacKenzie, Carter, Blackwater, and Russell. He confirmed they were there. MacKenzie and Blackwater are the ones who brought Mason to the hospital. MacKenzie even wrote Captain Mason's real name on the paperwork and proudly announced he was 5th Special Forces. They all sat in Mason's room in two-man shifts. An older man showed up a few days before Mason died. I don't have his identity."

"Considering Mason was dying, it could have been a friend or family member."

"What about Major Russell, sir?" Ortiz asked, waving his piece of paper. "Doesn't that show he knows something or is involved somehow?"

"Not really, Lieutenant. Those men survived a POW camp together. They probably called him, and he beat feet to get there in time. Did they say anything to the doctor about what they were doing in the area?"

"Camping, sir. The Salmon-Challis National Forest is nearby."

"Could be true. They can't exactly take a regular vacation at Disneyworld." Chris got an idea. "Did anything happen within, say, one hundred miles of that hospital?"

Ortiz smiled. "Yes, sir. The FBI arrested members of a militia group called the Freedom Revolution and recovered a missing truckload of Army weapons."

"The FBI, huh?" *Something tells me it wasn't the FBI. Chalk another mission up to Jackson and crew.*

"Yes, sir. Do you think MacKenzie was involved?"

"In what?" Chris wondered. "Recovering the weapons or stealing them?"

"Either one."

"Did you call the FBI?"

Ortiz nodded. "Yes. They told me no comment and to buzz off."

"Then my answer is no," Chris lied. He knew they helped the FBI recover the weapons. But if the FBI stayed silent, so would he. "I think it's a coincidence. They probably went camping."

"Is that how you want me to note it in my report?"

"Until we know otherwise, yes. We deal in facts, Lieutenant. I'm not a mind reader or a psychic, and neither are you. If the FBI didn't mention outside involvement in their case, it's not our problem. Carry on." Chris threw his used napkin in the trash can and went to his office. He felt sorry for Jackson and himself.

Now they'd lost two friends. First, Michael Roberts, even though they met for less than an hour. Now a man he knew for much longer. Captain Mason was an excellent officer, one he wanted under his command. It was a crying shame. Mason was destined for something other than a hole in the ground.

CHAPTER 31

1300 Hours
April 20, 1984
Building 54 – Nathan Hale Hall
902nd Military Intelligence Group Headquarters
Ft. Meade, MD

Lieutenant Ortiz burst into Chris' office. "Colonel, you need to look at this!"

Chris looked up, exasperated that Ortiz couldn't wait ten more seconds for him to finish reading this report. "What?"

Ortiz tossed a large, thick manila mailing envelope with the official Army seal broken on the desk. Stamped on the front under Colonel C. Patterson was *Eyes Only*. "This, sir."

"Are you developing a habit of reading my mail, Captain? This is addressed to me, not you." *That's not good if I get something important from my contacts.*

"No, sir." I got a call from the Pentagon to make sure you received it."

"And got curious?"

"Yes, sir."

Chris stood, placing his hands on the desktop. "That's all well and good, Lieutenant. Under normal circumstances, I would applaud you for your initiative…but this says *Eyes Only*, meaning mine. Not yours."

Ortiz looked at the ground. "Yes, sir. Aren't you going to take a look?"

"Later. I've got to finish reading these sighting reports about MacKenzie." *They're all bullshit like all the others unless he's taken to blowing up buildings in Europe. Even though demolition above and below the waterline was his specialty in 'Nam, not a chance.*

"Yes, sir." Ortiz appeared dejected as he left the office.

Chris wasn't sure why. It might have been the dressing down or the fact he didn't look at whatever was in the envelope. He pushed the envelope aside and went back to the reports. After signing the bottom of each to acknowledge receipt, he tossed the packet of reports into the outbox.

Getting curious about what had Ortiz excited like a boy in a girls' locker room, he pulled the paper-clipped bundle of papers out of the manila envelope. The title on the cover page – Grenada – Operation

Urgent Fury - Overview by ground officers involved in the conflict. U.S. Army, Navy, and Marine Corps. Meeting held 2 Dec 1983 - The Stardust – Las Vegas, NV.

Stamped at the bottom of the page – Reviewed by the Joint Chiefs of Staff - Part of the official record of Operation Urgent Fury.

Why would this get Ortiz excited? It was a comprehensive after-action report.

Chris flipped over the title page and skimmed the extensive document of words and charts. It covered operational planning, lack of preparation, map problems, the two failed SEAL missions, realistic training, a lack of an integrated communication system, and procedures for combining troops of different services.

Things boring to a young officer like Ortiz. However, as an experienced combat officer, Chris found the final synopsis interesting. Would eliminating one or more of those problems before the operation have a trickle-down effect? For example, could the casualty count – KIA or wounded (civilian, enemy, and allied forces) be far fewer than what we experienced? An excellent question.

Their answer – yes. The United States military was not ready for this action taken ten years after the withdrawal and subsequent military drawdown after Vietnam. While the victory in Grenada helped revive the American public's support of the military, as a combined operation regarding the command structure, it was a failure. The U.S Forces needed a unified command, not the splintered one used where the different branches didn't and couldn't talk to each other. More training along with enhancement of tactics and communications were needed.

That answer had to ruffle the feathers of more than a few command-grade officers involved in the operational planning.

He flipped to the last page to look at the list of officers involved in the report. One name caught his eyes – Colonel Jackson J. MacKenzie – U.S. Army – 5th Special Forces Group. Jackson took part in the discussion, and no one reported it. Probably because those officers didn't believe the bullshit. Good for them. At least there were a few. For it to be included in the official record must have stuck in the craw of those believing in Jackson's guilt. Mainly generals, the heads of a few government agencies, and whoever was involved in this ridiculous fiasco.

The question sure to come up from his commanding officer, General Manzarek - "What was he going to do about it?" His official answer – interview the officers on the list and find out what they know then type up a report. That meeting happened six months ago. Any leads were cold dead ends.

Unofficially, nothing. By taking part in the informal off-the-books conference, Jackson proved his conviction to his duty, patriotism, and loyalty to the United States. He made Chris proud to be his former friend. Maybe they could bury the hatchet and be friends again one of these days.

But until then, Chris had to maintain the illusion of doing his job when it came to anything involving Jackson. That included not looking into Jackson's insistence on being promoted to full colonel prior to the art museum mission. If it wound up true, he'd have to report what he found.

While that might eventually lead to the truth, he didn't want to wind up in JAG's crosshairs again, charged with Article 90 (Willfully Disobeying Superior Commissioned Officer) and 133 (Conduct Unbecoming an Officer). Once was enough. And he was guilty. The charges would stick this time. He'd better cross his fingers and hope he didn't get caught. The challenge made life worthwhile until he managed to run into Jackson again. He sure wasn't going to find him.

1715 Hours
April 25, 1984
Married Officers Housing
Ft. Meade, MD

Chris checked the mailbox on his way into the house. The envelope on top was a bill from MasterCard. Figuring the rest of the pile were bills or sales circulars, he didn't look through the rest. Their accumulated debt had doubled since they bought another car. The engine blew in their old one. It wasn't cost-effective to fix it. The loan put them in a big hole financially.

He entered the kitchen then placed his briefcase and mail on the table. Kara wasn't there, but something sure smelled good, enlightening his sour mood. The meaty aroma drifting through the house made his mouth water.

"Honey, I'm home," he yelled, checking the oven. Inside was a large roasting pot and a sheet pan of biscuits.

After pouring himself a cup of coffee from the pot, he went to the living room, turned on the TV, and sat in his chair to watch the news. He glanced over at the wet bar. No, he wouldn't do that.

Kara came in and knelt next to him. "How was your day?"

Chris sipped his coffee. "Long. Reports about the kidnapping of the CIA station chief in Beirut. India annexed more territory and moved into Siachen Glacier. The President's call for an international ban on chemical weapons. The list goes on and on. Nothing about Jackson. Those stopped after Grenada. The only thing I've seen about him was that after-action report I told you about."

"The one that rankled all your superiors?" Kara said, smiling, apparently loving every minute of the inside joke.

"Yes. They didn't know what to do with themselves other than yell at me and everyone else. Jackson showed his character as a soldier, and they showed theirs by being total assholes. My eval may be below average for the first time in my career. General Manzarek is a fu...freaking micromanaging prick. He wants a report about everything. Even on the stuff that is obviously a dead end."

Kara patted Chris' shoulder. "Sounds like it. Maybe you should retire."

"No. I've got to see this through. For both of us. The lack of information about Jackson worries me."

"How?"

"That Jackson might have had a setback." He had a hard time saying this. "Or he might be dead."

"Harry would have called you if that happened. Considering how bad you said he was hit, that's not surprising."

Chris appreciated her reassurance. "No, it isn't. When I interviewed Colonel Cord, he told me off the record Jackson almost died from a collapsed lung and would be out of commission for at least six months to maybe a year with a broken shoulder blade."

"There's your answer. He's healing."

"Yeah. I sure hope so." Chris gripped her hand. "What's for dinner?"

"Pot roast and biscuits. Now get your stuff off the table so we can eat."

"Great." Chris stood and stretched.

"I'm curious. What did Colonel Cord say on the record?" Kara asked.

Chris laughed. "That he believed Jackson was innocent. He invited him to the meeting because, as an outsider not involved in the planning, Jackson could give an unbiased opinion on the operation."

"He really said that? Isn't that a career killer?"

"For him, I doubt it. The guy's a rising star. I've heard he's a virtual lock at the next O-7 board. If I said that to the general, I'd be up on charges when he got back to his office."

They walked to the kitchen. Chris handed the mail to Kara then took his briefcase to the entry hall and set it next to the front door. He returned to the kitchen to set the table.

Kara waved an envelope. "Did you look at the mail?"

Chris shook his head. "No. Thought it was all bills. Why?"

"I think you should." She handed him a tattered, water-stained, yellowed envelope addressed to Lt. Colonel Christopher Patterson, 1st Battalion, 7th Regiment, 1st Cavalry Division, APO 96221 - Phước Vĩnh. The return address was obscured with either mud or blood.

The postmark over the stamp, August 25, 1970. Various other post markings were stamped on the envelope - Japan, Korea, San Diego, Fort Bragg. How typical of the Army mail system to be slow as molasses in December. But fourteen years? Who sent the letter to him? Why didn't he get it before today?

Chris slit open the envelope and pulled out a handwritten letter on lined white notebook paper.

08/24/70

Lt. Colonel Christopher Patterson
1st Battalion, 7th Regiment
1st Cavalry Division
APO 96221

Dear Chris,

I hope this letter finds you well. Thank you for the visit. You don't know what it meant to me to see your face after everything that happened to me in that POW camp. I don't know if I will ever be able to talk about it. It's hard to even think about it right now. I guess we'll see with time.

There were many days I wanted to die to end the pain, including here at the hospital those first few days. I was shocked to wake up alive in a hospital room after the evac chopper dropped us off. I don't know what the docs are going to recommend. My guess is I'm soon to be stateside bound and retired. That all depends on my recovery. If they allow me to remain in the Army, we need to get together and celebrate. All the drinks will be on me.

The food here sucks. I hope to move away from the pureed "baby food" and the NG tube soon and eat something more substantial with taste. The milkshakes can stay. Those I love. They must have it flown in because ice cream is hard to get in a war zone. Not that I am complaining. I can use the pampering. I'm lucky to be alive.

Keep your head down, Athos. Go home alive and make Kara happy. She deserves it. Maybe someday I'll find someone like her and have a family. Hold down the fort until my return. You'll always be my friend, no matter what happens. I need to sign off to get this in the evening mail run.

All for one and one for all.

Jackson MacKenzie
aka Aramis

Chris stared at the words – *You'll always be my friend no matter what happens*. Jackson wrote this on the day of his visit. Even though the fight occurred nearly a year later, those words still rang true in his soul.

"Who's it from?" Kara asked, startling Chris out of his revelry.

Chris handed her the letter, watching her reaction as she read it. A tear ran down her cheek.

"I don't even want to think about what they did to him," she said.

Chris brushed the tear away with his thumb. "Me neither. I've read about the torture techniques the NVA used on its prisoners. Waterboarding, whipping, solitary confinement, sweat boxes, tiger cages, the rope trick."

"What's that?"

"Are you sure you want to know?"

Kara nodded slowly. "Yeah, I need to know."

"They tie the prisoner's arms behind their back and rotate them upward until the shoulders and elbows pop out of their sockets. The ropes cut off circulation, causing numbness and muscle spasms. Sometimes, they hang them from the ceiling on a meat hook trussed up like that and beat them senseless."

"Oh my God!" Kara exclaimed. "Now his problems in the stockade make sense if they locked him in a tiger cage or solitary confinement. I had no idea they did things like that."

"Neither did I until I read the reports." *And according to Jackson's men, they did all those things and more to him.* Chris wasn't going to tell her that part, especially about the whipping that left Jackson's back scarred for life. "Jackson is still the man we know in our hearts." He needed to assure her as much as himself. *I hope. The torture probably changed him in ways we can't imagine.* The fight made more sense now than ever.

Given Chris' drinking problem, he'd probably be a pickled lush or dead if he had gone through the same things as Jackson.

"Why did the letter take so long to get to you?"

"The Army mail system isn't the greatest. It probably got lost from the number of postmarks." He shrugged. "Who knows?"

"Are you going to tell your superiors?" Kara asked.

"No!" Chris carefully placed the letter back into the envelope. "It's none of their business."

"Good."

"Getting this letter now does tell me one thing."

She gripped his hand. "What's that?"

Chris kissed her forehead. "Our friendship is worth saving. I'll figure out a way. Even if I lose my career over it." Duty above all else except honor. He was going to honor their friendship. Not even the horrors they saw in Vietnam or the Army's nonsense could succeed in destroying that bond. A bond formed in honorable service and their Rockbound Highland home in the hills above the Hudson River. West Point.

Made in the USA
Columbia, SC
25 October 2022

70016372R00093